BURIED TREASURES
OF THE
GREAT PLAINS

Books in W. C. Jameson's *Buried Treasures* series:

Buried Treasures of the American Southwest
Buried Treasures of the Ozarks
Buried Treasures of Texas
Buried Treasures of the Appalachians
Buried Treasures of the South
Buried Treasures of the Rocky Mountain West
Buried Treasures of California
Buried Treasures of the Pacific Northwest
Buried Treasures of the Atlantic Coast
Buried Treasures of New England
Buried Treasures of the Great Plains

BURIED TREASURES OF THE GREAT PLAINS

*Legends of Lost Immigrant Caches,
Abandoned Payroll Coins,
and Stagecoach Robbery Loot
–From North Dakota to Texas*

W.C. Jameson

August House, Inc.
ATLANTA

www.augusthouse.com

Printed in the United States of America

10 9 8 7 6 5 4 3 2

LIBRARY OF CONGRESS CATALOGING-IN-PUBLICATION DATA

Buried Treasures of the Great Plains / W. C. Jameson
p.   cm.
Includes bibliographic references
ISBN-13: 978-0-87483-486-4 (paper)
1. Great Plains—History, Local. 2. Treasure-trove—Great Plains.
3. Legends—Great Plains. I Title.
F591.J36 1997   96-45605
978-DC21   CIP

Executive editor: Liz Parkhurst
Project editor: Suzi Parker
Cover design and maps: Wendell E. Hall

The paper used in this publication meets the minimum requirements
of the American National Standards for Information Sciences—
permanence of Paper for Printed Library Materials, ANSI.48-1984

AUGUST HOUSE, INC. PUBLISHERS ATLANTA

Contents

I. Introduction 7

II. Kansas

The Choteau's Island Mystery   16
The Dalton Gang Loot   22
The Nemaha River Cache   29
The Spaniards' Forgotten Hoard   36
The Boarding House Treasure   40
Bill Doolin's Outlaw Gold   44
The Fate of the Chavez Gold   49

III. Nebraska

Spanish Gold at Plattsmouth   56
A Boy and His Train Robbery Loot   61
Scottsbluff Treasure Inn   66
The Lost $125,000 Army Payroll   71

IV. North Dakota

Missouri River Gold Cache   82
A Dreamer's Unlucky Fate   89
Treasure in the Well   95
Mysterious Chest of Gold Coins   99

V. Oklahoma

An Oklahoma Outlaw Stash   104
Buried Army Payroll at Fort Sill   113
The Hidden Mexican Gold Ingots   118
Cimarron County Gold Cache   123

VI. South Dakota

The *Monitor's* Stolen Fortune   132
The Central City Gold Shipment   140
A Hefty Gold Bar Robbery   144

VII. Texas

Sand Dunes Treasure   *154*

Incan Treasure on Salt Folk   *161*

The Rifle Pits   *171*

Lost Texas Ranger Treasure   *176*

Shafter Lake's Wagonloads of Gold   *181*

Glossary   187

Selected References   191

Introduction

"If you could locate and dig up all of the treasure that has been lost or
buried on the Great Plains, you would possess
greater wealth than Fort Knox."

These words, spoken to me several years ago by an old-timer who had lived all of his life on the Great Plains, initially seemed like an outrageous exaggeration. But after years of collecting and researching legends and tales of buried treasures in this vast, colorful, historic, and unique geographic area, I am inclined to agree with him.

When most people consider the subject of buried treasures, their thoughts generally run to locations such as those found in the Rocky Mountains, the Appalachians, maybe California, perhaps Arizona, sometimes Texas. Very few probably consider the Great Plains. It may be because that location doesn't, in the minds of many, possess the glamour, the adventure, and the romance associated with rugged and rocky mountain ranges and deep canyons, the gold-seeking forty-niners, or the Spanish conquest that, in part, was preoccupied with the discovery and mining of gold and silver. Some perceive the Great Plains as something less than spectacular, maybe even boring.

But to the surprise and delight of many, the Great Plains, actually a rather complex and varied environment, emerges as one of the most fertile regions in the United States for tales and legends of lost, hidden, and buried treasures. And the promise of an actual recovery of some incredible long lost fortune is as likely in this region as anywhere America, and perhaps greater.

Geographic Area

The Great Plains comprise a vast area located approximately in the middle of the United States and situated between the Rocky Mountains to the west, the Appalachian Mountains to the east, central Texas to the south, and the Canadian border to the north. This area, nearly the size of western Europe, contains about one-sixth of the United States' land mass, but less than five percent of its population. Though the Great Plains technically extend into Canada, this book will be concerned only with the portion that lies within the boundaries of the continental United States.

The Great Plains makes up most of the following states: North Dakota, South Dakota, Nebraska, Kansas, and large portions of Oklahoma and Texas. The easternmost parts of Montana, Wyoming, Colorado and New Mexico exhibit Great Plains topography, as do the westernmost portions of Minnesota and Iowa and the northwestern corner of Missouri.

The greatest percentage of American citizens know the Great Plains only from movie images. Many see it as a land of violent tornadoes, such as the one that carried Dorothy and Toto away, ravaging the Kansas and Oklahoma prairies. Some recall images of blowing topsoil accompanied by environmental desolation and human destitution as witnessed in *The Grapes of Wrath*. A few know only the comparatively bleak and endless landscapes in *Dances With Wolves*. Others remember the continuous and depressing wind and blowing tumbleweeds in *The Last Picture Show*.

Numerous perception surveys taken during the past twenty years indicate that, in the opinion of the majority of Americans, the Great Plains are a flat, somewhat featureless expanse of land located somewhere near the middle of the United States. Most perceive the Great Plains as limitless fields of wheat and other grains, possessing little or no topographic variation but having seemingly endless horizons.

Upon being enlightened about the landscape of the Great Plains, these same respondents are surprised to learn that this unique geographic region is anything but flat and featureless. Rolling hills, impressively deep, sculptured canyons, and even some surprising mountain ranges can be found in this vast, extensive region. The relief—the difference between highest and lowest points—in parts of Kansas, Oklahoma, and South Dakota is actually greater than in portions of the Ozark Mountains.

Origins

Geologically, the Great Plains were shaped by processes far different from those that were responsible for the formation of the Rocky, Appalachian, and Ozark mountain ranges. These prominent topographic features were composed of a variety of exposed rocks exhibiting impressive escarpments, deep stream-cut canyons, and, in some cases, exposed veins of precious ore. While the mountain ranges found on the North American continent are a result of various episodes of uplift, folding, faulting, and sometimes intensive volcanic activity, the Great Plains is characterized primarily by processes associated with deposition.

Despite a few relatively small mountain ranges found on the Great Plains, the majority of this environment was formed largely from the deposition of sediments carried by glacial meltwater. These sediments were later sculpted by the continuous processes of erosion generated by wind and flowing water.

On at least four different occasions during the Pleistocene, or Ice Age, which transpired approximately during the last one million years, huge glaciers nearly a mile thick grew and advanced across much of the North American continent, extending as far south as Kansas. The erosive power of these sheets of ice pushing along millions of tons of debris as part of their bed load smoothed out much of this region. The result of this scraping and abrading flattened exposed rock prominences. All of this caused much of the land to be leveled. After each major advance of the ice (scientists claim there were at least four, and some lasted as long as two hundred thousand years), the climate warmed enough to generate significant melting. As the ice sheets melted, the subsequent runoff covered the land for miles in all directions until it finally became channelized into the major drainage basins of the Mississippi, Missouri, Ohio, and other important rivers. As the sheets of water flowed across the landscape, they transported loads of fine sediment, much of which was deposited over great portions of the plains. In many cases, some of the finest agricultural lands found on the Great Plains today are associated with these rich, fertile soils.

When the last continental glacier finally receded more than 50,000 years ago, centuries of precipitation and runoff further modified the geographic character of the Great Plains. More and more channels that cut into the relatively soft soils and created deep gullies evolved to accommodate the runoff. Where the flowing water eroded through the sensitive underlying sandstones and limestones, impressive canyons were occasionally formed. These erosional processes continue today, providing ongoing forces that continue to alter the ever-changing dynamic character of the plains.

The People

During the 1700s, the population of the United States east of the Appalachian Mountains grew at a rapid rate as more and more people began to yearn for land and opportunities in the West. To the majority of citizens, the land west of the Mississippi River held a great mystery, and many became excited by the tales they heard from trappers who explored and hunted throughout the Rocky Mountains and California. These men returned with stories about the abundance of thick beaver pelts and lodes of precious minerals like gold and silver. In response to these tales, many Americans with an adventurous spirit traveled westward into the Rockies, blazing new trails across the Great Plains that would be followed by tens of thousands more migrants during succeeding decades. In crossing this wide expanse, the travelers and explorers noted the extensive herds of buffalo and the relative abundance of wild game, but in light of the potential fortunes, which many believed could be made in the western mountains, the prairies held no fascination for them. These extensive grasslands were considered little more than an obstacle with hazards—hostile Indians, occasional drought, and severe storms—that had to be crossed in order to get to a better place.

The initial lure of migrants to the Rocky Mountains soon dissipated. The once-plentiful beaver was all but completely trapped out except in the remotest of streams, and many hopeful trappers returned empty-handed. In addition, the bottom quickly dropped out of the market for the once-fashionable hats made from fine beaver fur; they were no longer in vogue.

Movement across the plains and into the Rocky Mountains and Pacific Coast slowed significantly until 1849. In the previous year, gold was discovered at Sutter's Mill, California. This event fueled desires for wealth in many eastern residents. As more and

11

more gold discoveries were made in California, thousands of Americans from the Middle Atlantic to the Lower South undertook the long journey to the gold fields. During the next few years, tens of thousands crossed the Great Plains on their long and often arduous journeys to the Golden State, thus lacing the prairie with a dense network of trails that were added to the older ones and would be followed by thousands more. Along these trails, small settlements sprang up where merchants catered to the needs of travelers and settlers. These settlements grew, prospered, and eventually became major cities on the Great Plains.

Many easterners, firmly believing that they needed only to arrive in California to become rich, often sold their personal property and withdrew their life savings in order to finance their westward journey. Some purchased fine wagons and sturdy oxen or mules, a few acquired durable horses to transport them across the vast, open land, and others of lesser means made the journey on foot, carrying only what they needed on their backs. Most of the migrants often had to abandon their belongings and personal wealth along the way.

Tales of Lost And Buried Treasure

Tales of lost and buried treasures often conjure up images of hard-rock mines of gold and silver, extensive shafts, and tunnels, which once yielded great quantities of precious metals. In truth, mines were rare on the Great Plains simply because exposed, ore-bearing bedrock was uncommon. But the Great Plains provided a setting for a different kind of treasure, which was, for the most part, carried into the region by migrants, settlers, soldiers, businessmen, and railroads. Much of this wealth, as a result of compelling and sometimes colorful circumstances, was subsequently lost or buried.

Many who transported their wealth with them from the east were often forced to abandon it at some point of the journey. The reasons were many: the heavy weight often slowed progress; wagons broke down and they, along with their contents, had to be abandoned; wagon trains were attacked. As the numbers of travelers increased along the many remote trails that laced the plains, the threat of Indian attack grew. The American Indian residents of the Great Plains—most notably the Arapaho, Kiowa, Comanche, Cheyenne, and Sioux—resented the intrusion of the great numbers of newcomers and often responded with an armed and hostile force intent on defending their homeland. The numbers of armed bandits and highwaymen also increased dramatically. Predation, robbery, and Indian attack became such common hazards along the many trails of the Great Plains that the military was eventually summoned into the area, adding another dimension to the lost and buried treasure history and folklore of the region.

Inevitably, with so many people moving back and forth across the Plains, some began to notice the abundance of prime agricultural land. Permanent settlement, based on farming, gradually increased, and with it many communities were established. As towns grew in size and wealth, banks were established and railroads connecting important population centers were constructed. With the banks and railroads came more outlaws and more robberies, soon followed by more lawmen and, eventually, more tales of lost and buried treasures.

Today, the Great Plains of North America is emerging as an important source of tales and legends of buried treasures and lost wealth. As interest in this subject increases, more and more scholars are collecting the tales and interviewing the natives, and greater activity centered around the search for many of these buried treasures is occurring. Amazingly, a few of these fabulous fortunes have actually been found.

The study of folklore, particularly buried treasure folklore, is experiencing a strong and active revival around the country. This pursuit, appropriately, is often concentrated on specific geographic regions in the country, regions which manifest certain and specific cultural characteristics.

The Great Plains of the United States, previously a relatively neglected area, is rising to the forefront of lost and buried treasure prominence. This book is an attempt to capture and provide some of the most interesting and intricately researched tales and legends that have come from this special and fascinating region.

KANSAS

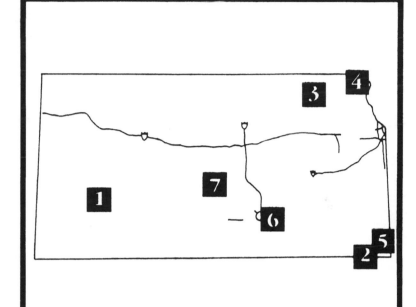

1. The Choteau's Island Mystery
2. The Dalton Gang Loot
3. The Nemaha River Cache
4. The Spaniard's Forgotten Hoard
5. The Boarding House Treasure
6. Bill Doolin's Outlaw Gold
7. The Fate of the Chavez Gold

The Choteau's Island Mystery

One of the greatest mysteries ever to perplex the residents of western Kansas concerns the location of Choteau's Island, a once-prominent landmark in the middle of the Arkansas River. And closely related to this mystery is another, perhaps more compelling one: What became of the huge fortune in silver coins that was buried on the island in 1828?

Choteau's Island, named after a prominent French fur trapper, was a large, forested sandbar located in the middle of the Arkansas River in Kearny County, Kansas, and considered an important landmark along the nearby Santa Fe Trail. During the spring of 1817, Choteau, the leader of a party of fellow French trappers, guided a pack train laden with valuable furs across Kansas to the markets in St. Louis, paralleling the Arkansas River since it was the most dependable water source in that part of the state. Around mid-afternoon one day, a large band of Pawnees, who resented the intrusion of the Frenchmen into their homeland, attacked the party. Not wishing to battle the fierce Indians on the open plain, Choteau spotted a long, tree-covered island in the middle of the river and signaled for his men to herd the mules onto it and take cover. For the next two days, the Frenchmen battled the Indians. Finally, the Pawnees rode away, carrying off more than one hundred of their dead and dozens more wounded, and the trappers, having lost only fifteen men, continued on their way toward St. Louis. The island was known thereafter as Choteau's Island.

Eleven years later, in August 1828, a party of traders and miners arrived in Santa Fe to refurbish their wagons and replenish supplies for a long journey to Independence, Missouri. The wagons contained furs from three seasons of successful trapping in the Rockies, but the most valuable cargo consisted of several dozen leather sacks filled with silver coins, accumulated during the preceding months from trapping, trading, and mining.

Despite warnings of hostile Indians preying upon travelers along the Santa Fe Trail, the twenty men, along with their five heavily loaded wagons and a herd of forty mules they hoped to sell in Missouri, pulled out of the city early one morning, anxious to reach their destination before cold weather set in.

Several weeks later, as the slow-moving caravan lumbered across the semiarid windy plains of western Kansas, a large Comanche war party appeared on the horizon. Nervously, the traders watched the Indians for nearly an hour, when without warning, the Comanches initiated an attack. Immediately, the traders responded by taking flight. Furiously whipping the teams that pulled the wagons and stampeding the close-herded mules down the trail, the travelers hoped to escape by outdistancing their pursuers.

The folly of this tactic was soon realized as John Means, the leader of the group, quickly observed the fast, sturdy Indian ponies closing in on the rather ponderous caravan. Means, along with three other men, turned back in an attempt to hold off the Indians with their revolvers, but as the wagons and mules thundered eastward, the four were set upon and killed instantly. As some of the warriors paused to scalp the victims, the remainder of the war party continued in pursuit of the fleeing traders.

One of the traders, acting on a hunch, turned the mules off the trail and herded them in a different direction. As he expected, the

Indians followed the animals and ignored the five escaping wag-ons.

The traders put as much distance between themselves and the Indians as possible before stopping for the night. Of the twenty-five horses remaining, seven dropped dead from exhaustion within an hour, and two more had to be destroyed because of serious wounds or injuries.

Around the campfire that evening, Lawson Beatty, a veteran of several skirmishes with Comanches, informed the men that once the mules had been gathered up and returned to their camp the Indians would likely resume pursuit of the wagon train for the goods they believed were being transported. Suspecting the Indi-ans cared more for the supplies in the wagons than the scalps of the traders, the men abandoned the vehicles at this site, loaded only the bags of silver coins and some food onto the few good horses that remained, and planned to continue on to Missouri in the morning.

At dawn the following day, the men decided to tie four of their horses to the wagons in the hope they would help appease the Comanches. The rest were packed, and shortly after sunrise, the severely depleted party continued eastward toward Missouri.

Finding no game along the way, the men were occasionally forced to kill one of the horses for meat. One evening, while the exhausted travelers were sleeping, a pack of wolves frightened away the remaining horses. When the men awoke the next morning, they discovered the loss of the animals and realized they were now on foot.

Hoisting the heavy packs of silver coins, they trudged along the trail, much slower and more discouraged than before, and for three more days they lugged the heavy burdens. When they finally arrived at the Arkansas River, the men decided it would be prudent to cache the coins in a secret place and return for them after procuring some wagons.

Recognizing Choteau's Island in the middle of the river, the weary travelers waded the stream and camped within the forested confines. On their second day on the island, they excavated a large hole, deposited the sacks of silver specie into it, and refilled it. Atop the large cache, they rolled a heavy boulder to mark the site. Several of the men scratched their names onto the large rock. After resting for awhile on the island, they continued their trek with four hundred miles still separating them from their destination.

For days the men, now weakened by their efforts and from the lack of food and water, followed the trail. Before long, several grew too weak to continue, and five of the strongest volunteered to proceed and try to find help. When the five finally arrived at Independence, they immediately organized a rescue party and returned for their comrades. By the time they reached the traders, several had already perished and the survivors were starved and half-crazed.

Because of the horrible experiences they endured along the Santa Fe Trail, the survivors of the ordeal never returned to Choteau's Island to recover the buried cache of silver. In the telling of the incredible tale of escape and survival during the succeeding years, however, the traders interested others in the prospect of locating and retrieving the fortune in silver coins, and before long an expedition was organized to enter Comanche country to find Choteau's Island.

Arriving at the banks of the Arkansas River from where Choteau's Island was normally seen, the search party was surprised to discover it was no longer there. For days they rode up and down the river searching for the long strip of forested island on which the treasure was buried, but to no avail. Choteau's Island had disappeared.

For many years, others came and searched for the island but were likewise unable to locate it, and presently the story of the lost silver faded from people's thoughts and was remembered dimly by only a few old-timers.

Recent studies, however, have revealed that Choteau's Island has not disappeared at all. Instead, it has simply been relocated as a result of a change in the course of the Arkansas River.

According to a researcher employed by the National Park Service, the Arkansas River jumped its banks and established a new course in the region of Choteau's Island during severe flooding around 1830. The former island is no longer an island at all, but part of the adjacent floodplain.

Most who were familiar with the tale of buried treasure on the island were convinced it would be impossible to relocate the cache, but interest in the buried coins was revived in 1931 when the large rock that was rolled atop the hoard to mark it was accidentally discovered. In that year, a photograph appeared in a Colorado newspaper showing several members of a Kansas farm family posing next to a large boulder. The photograph was taken in the middle of a corn field located next to the Arkansas River in Kearny County, Kansas. Several French names etched into the rock's surface could clearly be seen in the photograph. An alert reader, knowledgeable of the tale of the buried silver coins, contacted the photographer and obtained a vague set of directions to the location of the rock. For two weeks, he traveled up and down the river in Kearny County searching for the boulder but had no success. Some claimed the corn was too high to be able to view the rock; others suggested that deposition of sand and mud from a recent flood may have covered the boulder. In any case, it has never been found.

Continual and patient research into what became of Choteau's Island could yield impressive results, for buried somewhere on the former strip of land once located in the middle of the Arkansas River is a fortune in silver coins.

The Dalton Gang Loot

Many who study the history of the American West are familiar with the Dalton Gang and their numerous outlaw deeds. The final act of the gang— the attempted robbery of two banks at the same time in Coffeyville, Kansas—led to the death of four members and the eventual end to their reign of terror and holdups. Hundreds of books and magazine articles have been written and a score of films made about the Daltons and the Coffeyville Raid. What very few people are aware of, however, is the fortune in gold and silver coins buried by the outlaws on the evening before the robberies. This cache is estimated to be between $9,000 and $20,000 in 1892 values.

The Dalton Gang had been formulating plans to rob the two banks in Coffeyville for months. Emmett, Bob, and Grat Dalton, along with friends Dick Broadwell and Bill Power, comprised the gang that had already earned a reputation as one of the most daring and dangerous in the Great Plains. Only Frank and Jesse James and their motley band of followers ever achieved more notoriety, but Jesse had been dead for ten years—shot by Robert Ford in 1882—and Frank had retired from outlawry and was leading a respectable life. Even Jesse James never robbed two banks at the same time.

Somehow, word reached Coffeyville that the Daltons intended to make a raid on the town's two banks, and the citizens of that otherwise quiet community armed themselves against such an event. Learning this, Emmett and Bob decided to wait a few months, assuming all the while that the residents would lose interest and forget about them. In the meantime, the bandits busied themselves with other robberies. They held up a Missouri, Kansas, and Texas train near Wagoner, Oklahoma, and another near Adair. From these two holdups they netted, it is believed, about $10,000. A few weeks later, they walked into another Oklahoma bank in El Reno about an hour before it opened and forced a startled teller to hand over $17,000.

From this money, most Dalton Gang scholars believe the outlaws spent no more than $2,000 or $3,000 on some new saddles and clothes. In the few days before the planned Coffeyville raid, many believe the outlaws carried just a little more than $20,000 in their saddlebags, though some claim it was considerably less, closer to $9,000.

On October 1, 1892, the Dalton Gang gathered at Tulsa to finalize their plans for the assault on Coffeyville. When they were ready, they started out toward their intended target—nearly sixty miles to the north-northeast. On the evening of October 5, they arrived at Onion Creek near where it confluences with the Verdigris River close to the Kansas-Oklahoma border. They set up camp, and, intending to travel as unencumbered as possible, unloaded all excess goods from their horses. The $20,000 in gold and silver coins they carried collectively was placed in a shallow hole adjacent to their campsite.

At dawn the following morning, the outlaws ate breakfast, checked their firearms and ammunition, and saddled their mounts. Just before riding from the campsite, Emmett Dalton told the gang members that if they became separated they were to rendezvous at this same Onion Creek campsite where they would recover the buried cache and escape deeper into Oklahoma.

At 9:30 A.M., the bandits rode into Coffeyville. Many historians claim six gang members entered the town, but this has never been verified. As shopkeepers swept the walks in front of their stores and citizens began the day's activities, the horsemen rode casually down the main street and up to a hitching post ironically located in front of the home of Judge Munn. Seated upon their mounts at this location, they could see the two banks they intended to rob—the First National Bank and the C.M. Condon and Company Bank.

After tying their horses to the hitch rail, Bob and Emmett Dalton approached the First National Bank while Grat Dalton, Broadwell, and Power walked toward the Condon Bank. The bandits were completely unaware they were being observed by several citizens who had grown suspicious of the quiet appearance of three newcomers. As the bandits approached the banks, they pulled revolvers from their holsters, and at that point, several of the observers armed themselves while others sped through the town warning residents and businessmen. Town Marshall Charles T. Connelly was notified of the strangers' arrival and their intentions, and he alerted his deputies. Within minutes, dozens of armed citizens and lawmen were watching the two banks from shop windows, shaded alleys, and the rooftops.

About fifteen minutes later, the bandits had filled several sacks with coins and currency and prepared to make a dash toward the tethered horses. As they exited the wide front doors of each bank, they were surprised by the thunder of gunfire as the townspeople opened fire on the bandits. With bullets kicking up dust all around them, they hesitated only a moment before attempting to sprint toward their horses. Grat Dalton was the first of the outlaws to be killed when Marshall Connelly gunned him down. As Grat fell, however, he fired a fatal shot at the lawman, striking him squarely in the chest.

The crowd of armed citizens grew to more than one hundred, and into their midst ran Bill Power, carrying several heavy sacks of coins and currency and trying to reach his horse. The crowd was so dense that Power had to literally fight his way through the throng. It was only a matter of time before he was killed; more than a dozen bullets pierced his body. As Power fell, he dropped the sacks of money, spilling coins all over the ground.

As Coffeyville citizens Lucius Baldwin and George Cubine ran to the aid of Marshall Connelly, they were both shot and killed by Dick Broadwell. Dropping the money bags he carried, Broadwell made it across the crowded street to his horse. Even though he was shot several times, he managed to climb into the saddle and flee from town. Several men immediately mounted up and went in pursuit.

The moment Bob and Emmett Dalton heard the gunfire and saw the huge crowd, they turned and ran out the back door of the First National Bank. Approaching the same door from the alley was a group of heavily armed men led by Charles Brown. Bob Dalton raised his pistol and shot Brown in the forehead, killing him instantly. The men behind Brown opened fire, and the impact of the shells knocked Bob to the ground and severely wounded Emmett. In spite of having been struck by at least a dozen bullets, Emmett fought his way through the group of men, around the building, and across the street to his horse. Leaping into the saddle, he rode back to the alley in an attempt to rescue Bob. In the process, Emmett received another dozen wounds. As he tried to pull his brother onto the horse, Bob was shot in the back and killed. In the next few seconds, Emmett was struck several more times, finally falling from his horse.

Meanwhile, Dick Broadwell, gushing blood from a dozen wounds and out his mouth, rode about a mile out of town before falling from his saddle. When a half-dozen Coffeyville defenders reached him, he was dead.

As the gun smoke began to clear, townsfolk saw sacks of money and spilled coins scattered among the fallen outlaws. Cautious and with guns at the ready, the citizens approached the bank robbers. All were dead except for Emmett Dalton. Amazingly, and in spite of receiving a total of twenty-seven bullet wounds, he was alive.

The next day as Emmett Dalton recovered on a cot in the office of the town's physician, his companions were being buried in Coffeyville's Elmwood Cemetery. Despite his numerous gunshot wounds and loss of blood, Emmett Dalton recovered only to be tried for his part in the robbery, convicted, and sentenced to a life term in the Kansas State Prison.

Emmett Dalton was regarded as a model prisoner and served only fifteen years behind bars when he was pardoned in 1907. Several lawmen believed that Dalton, once freed, would lead them to the coin cache at the Onion Creek campsite. They followed him for several months after he was released from prison, but to no avail. Dalton eventually moved to Tulsa, took a job as a security officer, and later opened a butcher shop.

It was soon obvious to the former outlaw that he was being tailed everyplace he traveled, so he stayed away from Onion Creek, intending to return only when he was certain his trackers had tired of trailing him.

A few years later, Emmett Dalton moved to Hollywood, California, where he served as a consultant with the film industry, even appearing in a film entitled *When the Daltons Rode*. Many people close to Emmett Dalton claimed the outlaw significantly changed his ways and sought only to live a life of peace and harmony. Many stated that the former outlaw often expressed that he was truly sorry for his past outlaw deeds and vowed to change his life for the good. As a result, Dalton Gang historians suggest that Emmett perceived the buried treasure at Onion

Creek as tainted and wanted nothing more to do with the ill-gotten gains. As far as anyone knows, it has never been recovered.

The exact location of the Onion Creek campsite has been disputed over the years, but recently discovered information has narrowed the area of search.

On the day before riding into Coffeyville, the bandits were seen riding onto the P.L. Davis Ranch located near the state boundary just outside the town of South Coffeyville. After passing in front of the Davis residence, they rode across a freshly plowed field and into a dense thicket of trees on the west bank of Onion Creek. After getting a small fire started to make some coffee, two of the outlaws rode to a nearby farm owned by J.F. Savage to purchase some grain for their horses.

Shortly after dawn the following morning, Mary Brown, the young daughter of another nearby rancher, was riding her horse when she heard voices near Onion Creek. Pulling her mount to a halt, she listened intently and overheard the sounds of men eating breakfast and saddling horses. A few minutes later, according to Mary Brown, five horsemen came riding out from under the small wooden bridge that spanned the creek. As she sat on her horse, she watched the men gently gallop toward Coffeyville.

Many years later when Mary Brown was an adult, she heard the story of the $20,000 being buried near the creek. She realized the outlaw campground had been near the bridge and believed she could find it. During the time that had passed since the Coffeyville Raid, however, the old bridge had been torn down, the road had been relocated, and portions of the creek had changed course. Though she examined the area for a full day, she was unable to identify the place where she had observed the Dalton Gang so many years earlier.

The gold and silver coins, according to researchers, are still buried somewhere on Onion Creek near the Kansas-Oklahoma state line.

The Nemaha River Cache

The news of the discovery of gold at Sutter's Mill, California, in 1848 started a mass migration of thousands toward the Rocky Mountains and the West Coast. Most who made the long journey west in search of riches came away disappointed. The few who possessed fair patience and persistent endurance were often rewarded with discoveries of the precious ore.

Two young men arrived in the Rocky Mountains from Boston, Massachusetts, in 1850. When they originally heard of the gold ading west to try and find their fortunes in the grudging rock of the mountains, but they were intimidated by the great distance and the long journey. Eventually, however, their dreams of wealth exerted a stronger pull than their fear of the unknown land between them and their destiny. They sold everything they owned, bought a pair of horses, and undertook the long and difficult voyage.

Four months later they arrived in California, surprised at the large numbers of people already there. For weeks, they explored the mountain ranges, but everywhere they went they encountered miners digging the precious metal from the shafts and panning it from the numerous glacially fed streams that tumbled from the high, snow-covered peaks through the dark, forested canyons.

Eventually the two young men found a canyon that other miners had not yet discovered. They set up a primitive camp and set out to find whether or not there was any gold in the nearby stream.

Their initial efforts went unrewarded, but maintaining a positive feeling about the area, they persisted until, after about six weeks of patient and consistent panning, they struck gold. It was only a few tiny nuggets at first, but with continued effort, their take grew slightly larger with each passing day.

Five years of panning gold in the narrow stream eventually yielded an impressive amount of ore. Each day, the two men placed the results of their efforts into an old gunpowder keg they kept for that purpose. As the keg gradually filled, they began to reminisce about their days together in Boston, their families, and about all the things they missed about their hometown. Eventually, their homesickness grew to be almost overwhelming and they often thought about packing up and returning home.

One morning in the spring of 1855, they completely filled the keg with gold nuggets and decided it was time to depart. After traveling to the nearest settlement, they purchased a wagon, a fresh pair of horses, and some supplies. At the same time, they encountered a caravan of traders preparing to return to St. Louis. The leader of the pack train told the two miners they were welcome to ride along with them for as far as they wished.

For weeks, the slow-moving train of mules, horses, oxen, and wagons wound through steep mountain passes and across the seemingly endless prairie. Indians were occasionally spotted, but the large size of the caravan discouraged attack.

Each night as the pack train stopped for camp, several of the mule skinners indulged in drinking and gambling that lasted long into the night. The two miners cared little for such activities and distanced themselves as much as possible from the group. Before long, a few of the mule skinners learned that the two newcomers were transporting a keg filled with gold nuggets and attempted to lure them into games of chance. Growing more and more concerned about their safety and that of the gold, as well as growing impatient with the extremely slow progress of the train, the partners decided to separate from the caravan and made their own way across the plains.

After leaving Julesburg, Nebraska, the two men guided their wagon along an eastward course toward the Missouri River. Several days later, running low on supplies and weary from long days of travel, they arrived at the small settlement of Richmond, located in the northern part of what is now known as Nemaha County, Kansas.

Richmond was a new trading center located on the west bank of the north-south oriented Nemaha River. The town was only six months old at the time the two travelers arrived and consisted of mercantile stores, a blacksmith shop, a livery, and nearly a dozen lumber and canvas structures serving as cafes, saloons, and gambling parlors. The largest building in the town, located on the west bank of the river, was a combination restaurant, saloon, and gambling casino.

Passing through the young town, the men arrived at the river, forded it, and set up camp on the opposite bank with the intention of returning to town later for a bath and shave, a hot meal, and supplies. About forty yards from where the two men busied themselves erecting their tent and staking out their tired horses, a family bustled about preparing dinner around a campfire. Presently, a man rose from a log where he sat and walked over to speak with the two miners. He introduced himself as William Ripley, a trader, and he said he was traveling with his wife and two daughters. After exchanging a few pleasantries, Ripley returned to his campsite.

Because the two men did not wish to lug the heavy keg of gold around on their short trip back into town and since they intended to remain at this location for about a week, the two friends decided to bury their fortune. When darkness arrived, they selected a spot slightly illuminated by the glare of the big saloon's lights, which shined thorough the fork of a large cottonwood tree growing near the river's bank. There, they excavated a hole about three feet deep, lowered the keg into it, and covered it with dirt, branches, and leaves. This done, they climbed aboard the wagon and rode into town.

Both the two young miners and the Ripley family remained at this campsite for about a week, and during that time, the two groups became well acquainted with each other.

On the evening prior to their planned date of departure, the two miners decided to go back to Richmond, pick up a few more supplies, and take one final meal in the cafe. After obtaining a shave and bath, acquiring supplies, and loading them into the wagon, the two miners parked in front of the large saloon near the river. After entering it, they took a table near one wall and ordered dinner. As they ate, they heard the shouts and laughter of several men gambling in the large room attached to the rear of the building.

Presently, a small group of men, obviously drunk, spilled out of the back room and into the cafe. Boisterous and aggressive, they shoved customers aside as they made their way toward the bar. The two diners immediately recognized the men as the mule skinners that were employed by the large wagon train. When one of the mule skinners spotted the two travelers, he walked over to their table and asked them where their gold was. When the two refused to respond, the mule skinner turned the table over and began beating on one of them. When the other tried to protect his friend, the mule skinner pulled out a gun and shot him in the face, killing him instantly.

As the cafe erupted into a free-for-all, the surviving miner fought free of the clutches of the mule skinner and ran outside. Leaping upon the wagon seat, he whipped the horses across the

Nemaha River ford and fled eastward into the night, not stopping at the campsite to retrieve any of his goods or the gold. Two days later he arrived in St. Joseph, Missouri, and shortly thereafter arranged for transportation back to Massachusetts.

Once back in Boston, the young man found work and settled into the everyday business of living. Though his thoughts were often on the keg of gold nuggets buried near the Nemaha River in the Kansas Territory, he feared to return. Years passed, and he married a young lady and fathered two sons.

When the Civil War broke out, the miner enlisted. Just before leaving with his regiment, he spoke with his wife and sons, telling them the story of what happened at the Richmond tavern and about the huge cache of gold. He even drew a map showing the location of the campsite on the river's east bank, the cottonwood tree, and the site where the keg was buried. When he returned from the war, he said, he wanted to travel to Kansas, retrieve the gold, and return to Boston a wealthy man. A year later he was killed in a skirmish with the Confederate Army in Virginia.

The widow raised the two sons and saw to their education, and as they grew to manhood, she reminded them of the story of their father's buried gold in Kansas. In 1883, the two sons, now young men, set out for Richmond, Kansas, on a quest to find the gold and bring it to Boston.

On arriving, they were surprised to discover that the town of Richmond no longer existed, only a single caved-in rock cistern marked the location of this once-thriving settlement. Riding to Seneca, a settlement located about two miles to the south, they learned that Richmond had been abandoned and torn down.

Returning to the location of the former town, the sons scanned the banks of the Nemaha River for some sign of the campsite as described by their father, but their gaze met only cleared and cultivated farmland. The ford across the river from Richmond to

33

the campsite was easily found, but the grove of trees that marked the campground had long since been cut down. The cottonwood that stood near the site where the keg of gold had been buried was gone.

Though the brothers dug and poked around in the ground along the bank for several hundred yards in either direction, they found nothing. Discouraged, they returned to Boston.

One day in 1905, an old man arrived in Seneca and inquired about the location of the old town of Richmond. For the next few days, passers-by often spotted him digging holes in the field on the east side of the Nemaha River opposite from the former town of Richmond.

After about two weeks of such digging, the old man returned to Seneca, where he made friends with a few residents. One of his new friends was W.F. Thompson, the editor of the Seneca newspaper. The old man eventually told Thompson the reason he had come to the area.

Always interested in the history of the region, the old man had learned of the killing of the young miner from Massachusetts in 1855 during a barroom scuffle. It was believed by many, according to the visitor, that before meeting his death, the young man, along with a partner, had buried a sizeable fortune in gold nuggets that was being transported across the prairie in a powder keg nearby.

The old man told Thompson that in 1855 he had been camped with his family on the east bank of the river across from Richmond that very night and had spoken with the young man who was killed. He introduced himself to the newspaper editor as William Ripley.

During the previous months, Ripley, while tracking down the story of the buried gold, had made contact with the widow and the two sons of the surviving miner. He learned about their fruitless search for the buried treasure and how the land around the old town of Richmond had changed. But he believed that because he had once camped on the east bank of the Nemaha River opposite the town he would be in a better position to find the gold. The widow agreed to let Ripley have the map providing he would share the treasure with the family should it be found.

In a few days, dozens of people were aware of Ripley's purpose for being in town, and soon the field just east of the river swarmed with treasure hunters, all digging holes in the ground. Soon afterward, the owner of the property evicted everyone and posted NO TRESPASSING signs. Ripley, along with Thompson, tried to gain access to the land but was denied. Ripley died shortly afterward.

Several who have studied and researched the tale of the buried powder keg filled with gold nuggets near Seneca claim that the wooden staves and lids would have rotted away long ago, and that the gold was likely mixed with the adjacent soil. Some have suspected that years of tilling and plowing in this region may have churned up some of the gold, mixing it with the arable soil on the surface.

It never seemed likely that this huge cache of gold, buried a century and a half earlier, might be at or near the surface of the ground, but an event occurred in 1917 that has many people believing it could have happened. For years, area residents hunted ducks up and down the Nemaha River. The birds were easily shot as they grazed on the grain remaining on the ground from the previous season's harvest. One day, a farmer named Potts shot two ducks grazing in the field opposite the old town of Richmond. Taking them home that afternoon, he plucked them and gave them to his wife to clean for dinner. To her amazement, the stomachs of both birds contained tiny gold nuggets!

The search continues.

The Spaniards' Forgotten Horde

Sometime during late spring in 1736, a party of seven Mexicans established a temporary camp about a mile from the west bank of the Missouri River at a location somewhere between the present-day towns of Highland and Sparks in Doniphan County, Kansas. Arriving at the river several days earlier, the travelers found it in flood and far too high and swift to cross with their unwieldy ox carts and heavily laden burros. Anticipating a long wait before the waters receded, the Mexicans retreated to a thin grove of trees a short distance away, set up camp, and allowed their animals to graze on the rich prairie grasses growing in profusion nearby.

The Mexicans had been several weeks on the trail after departing from the Rocky Mountains near Denver, Colorado. Deep in the mountains, the reclusive men worked for seven years, spending as much as fourteen hours a day, seven days a week, in their mines extracting the precious gold ore from the rock. Near the end of the seventh year, they collectively decided they had accumulated as much gold as they needed, so they took their ore to Denver, converted it to coins, and departed for St. Louis. At St. Louis, they intended to book passage on a steamboat down the Mississippi River to New Orleans and then travel by ship to Mexico where they would retire in luxury. After seven long years of working in the mines and living in the wilderness, a few days of camping on the Great Plains while waiting for the river to drop was nothing, and the men passed their time hunting, sleeping, and playing cards.

On the afternoon of the third day in camp, the Mexicans spotted a group of twelve riders, all leading fully loaded pack horses, approaching from the west. Warily, they eyed the newcomers as they rode toward the camp, and when the riders were still about a hundred yards away, the Mexicans recognized them as trappers transporting a load of furs to St. Louis. The Mexicans offered to share their campsite with the new arrivals, but the surly trappers rode a short distance away and established their own camp.

Later that same day, one of the trappers came to the Mexicans' camp and demanded liquor. When told there was none, he grew belligerent and picked a fight with the nearest man. Quickly subdued by the other six, the trapper angrily stalked back to his camp where he told his companions about the encounter. As the Mexicans watched, the trappers pulled out their flintlocks and began charging them with powder.

Expecting an attack from the trappers, the Mexicans armed themselves with the few pitiful weapons at their disposal—a pair of old pistols and a rusted blunderbuss. Concerned that the trappers might discover their fortune in gold coins, the Mexicans quickly excavated several holes where they placed their fortunes. Several metal boxes contained the coins, and all of them were buried throughout the campsite.

The fears of the Mexicans were realized. By the time they had covered the last box, the trappers were advancing on the camp, rifles at the ready.

For the next half-hour, the two groups exchanged shots, but the superior numbers and firepower of the trappers finally prevailed and eventually all of the Mexicans were killed. After rifling through the ox carts and finding little worth taking, the trappers burned them. Then, they gathered all of the Mexican's livestock and returned to their camp. Two days later, they crossed the river.

Just a few inches below the surface of the prairie at the camp the trappers had destroyed lay what many believe is a fortune in gold ore amounting to nearly $1 million in today's values. The gold would probably have remained lost and forgotten had it not been for a significant event that occurred in 1891.

During the early 1880s, a man named G.G. Fox settled a section of land in Doniphan County on which he planted corn and wheat. Initially, Fox lived in a sod house, but as the years passed and his farm prospered, he constructed a fine home and barn of milled lumber.

In 1891, Fox decided to build an icehouse on his property, so he selected a suitable location and began to dig a large, rectangular hole not far from his house. Within the first minute of digging, Fox's shovel struck something metallic, and when he paused to investigate, he discovered a rusted metal box. When he opened the box, he was astonished to find it filled with gold coins.

Fox placed the metal box of gold coins in the bed of his wagon and rode into Highland. After showing his find to the manager of the local bank, he learned that it was worth several thousand dollars. Suddenly, Fox was very wealthy, and as he was nearing sixty-five years of age, he decided to quit farming, move to Kansas City, and live a comfortable life. Fox never considered that there might be more gold buried on his property. He simply abandoned his farm and was never seen in Doniphan County again.

Time passed, the old farmer's house and barn rotted away, and the Fox farm was eventually taken over by others. None of the new tenants, however, were aware of the buried cache of gold coins.

Today, very little is known about the old farm or where the original house and barn stood. If the actual sites of these structures could be determined, the location of Fox's planned icehouse could likely be found. A fortune in gold coins, worth millions, awaits some lucky person.

The Boarding House Treasure

Today, Galena, Kansas, is a quiet town of approximately three thousand five hundred people located in the southeastern part of the state near the Missouri border. More than a hundred years ago, however, this area was the site of a lead mining boom where dozens, probably hundreds, of men grew wealthy in a relatively short time. Because of the large amounts of money they carried around, many of these men met death as a result of one woman's greed and lust for wealth. It is estimated that tens of thousands of dollars' worth of gold and silver coin and currency were taken from the bodies of her victims and buried in a secret location. Before she was able to spend her accumulated fortune, the woman was arrested and sent to prison where she spent the rest of her life.

Galena lies on the northwestern edge of a portion of the Ozark Mountains that extend only a few miles into southeastern Kansas. During the mid-1800s when thousands of Americans were making the long journey to California following the discovery of gold in that state, lead was discovered in what would eventually become Cherokee County, Kansas. But it was several years before the area experienced a mining boom, because lead was not nearly as valuable as gold and the region was relatively unoccupied. As demand for the metal grew, however, more and more people filtered into the region to prospect for and mine the lead. Soon, the area was filled with seekers combing the hills, searching for a major lead strike. And lead was found everywhere: exposed rock formations housed great quantities of it; local farmers claimed their mule-drawn plows turned it up in huge quantities in the fields; it was even found clinging to the roots of plants when they were yanked from the soil. Almost overnight, penniless prospectors became millionaires.

As the mines were opened and hundreds of men found work, a small community of tents sprang up nearby. As it grew and permanent buildings were constructed, a town was founded and called Galena in honor of the bluish-grey lead sulphide found in abundance throughout the region. As the town grew, mercantile shops opened, churches were built, and saloons could be found on nearly every street corner.

As business prospered and the wealth in Galena grew at an astonishing rate, one enterprising woman named Steffleback decided to obtain some of it. After observing the great numbers of miners, prospectors, engineers, and businessmen arriving in town each day, she decided to capitalize on what she perceived as an excellent opportunity. After selecting a suitable piece of land, Steffleback constructed a two-story house with several rooms and opened a bordello.

In a very short time, Steffleback's house became the most popular place in town. Around sundown, the bordello filled with heavy-drinking prospectors and miners, their pockets bulging with proceeds from recent business deals.

Steffleback grew quite wealthy during the next few years, but she was never completely satisfied with the rate that she accumulated her money. With a burning desire to become the wealthiest woman in Kansas, she decided it would be quicker and easier to kill the patrons and rob them of their coin and cash.

One evening, a local miner sat alone at a table drinking whiskey. Steffleback noticed he paid for his drinks by pulling gold coins from a heavy leather sack tied to his belt. She estimated the sack contained several thousand dollars.

About two hours later when the customer was quite drunk, Steffleback lured him into a back room and sat him down in a chair. As she stood before the inebriated man and engaged him in conversation, one of her sons sneaked up behind him and split his head open with an axe. Quickly, Steffleback took the victim's purse and later, when no one was about, the son stuffed the dead miner into a canvas bag, loaded him onto a horse, and carried him to an abandoned mine shaft where his body was deposited.

Surprised and delighted at the ease with which the robberies could be carried out, Steffleback lured as many as twenty-five or thirty victims into her back room during the next few years. Most of those killed and robbed were drifters and had no close ties to anyone in town. On the rare occasions when someone was reported missing, most people presumed the individual had simply packed up and left town.

Steffleback, in an effort to minimize suspicion on herself, lived somewhat frugally, constantly complaining loud enough for all to hear that she never had enough money to pay her bills. Steffleback distrusted banks, but more importantly, she refused to deposit her fortune in one because she didn't want anybody to be aware she had wealth. Meanwhile, it is estimated her share of the robberies amounted to tens of thousands of dollars.

As Steffleback grew increasingly wealthy, she never revealed where she hid her money to anyone, not even her sons. She rarely left the sporting house, and many presumed she buried it nearby.

One evening, Steffleback and one of her prostitutes became involved in a heated argument concerning a customer. In a fit of anger, Steffleback fired the girl and had her thrown out into the street. Seeking revenge, the young woman went immediately to the sheriff and informed him of her former employer's murderous activities. The next day, Steffleback was arrested.

While awaiting trial, the bordello was searched thoroughly for Steffelback's hoard of coins and currency but nothing was ever found. A search of several abandoned mine shafts, however, yielded the bodies of at least a dozen of her victims.

During the trial, Steffleback refused to admit guilt or reveal where she had hidden her fortune. In 1897, she was found guilty and sentenced to life in the state women's prison in Lansing.

W.H. Haskell, the prison warden, was instructed by authorities to monitor Steffelback's tenure in prison. It was assumed by many that she would break down under the stress of confinement and reveal the location of her hidden wealth. The former madam was convinced that she would not remain in jail for long and launched a series of appeals, none of which were given serious consideration. Finally, on a cold day in March 1909, Steffleback died and carried her secret to the grave.

Following Steffleback's death, the story of her missing hoard was revived and printed in area newspapers. Soon, treasure hunters and curiosity seekers visited Galena. Some came from as far away as Colorado. Many treasure hunters concentrated their searches on the old bordello; floors were ripped up and walls pulled down, but nothing was ever found. Several local residents were convinced that Steffleback had hidden her treasure in some of the old abandoned lead mines. This was an unlikely consideration because the woman seldom left her property, and a search of the mines turned up nothing.

A few who claim to have thoroughly researched the story of Steffleback's treasure are convinced it is buried somewhere in the yard that once surrounded the old bordello. If one should be able to identify the structure's former location, a thorough examination of the adjacent grounds could possibly yield a fortune in coin and currency that could, at today's values, exceed $200,000.

Bill Doolin's Outlaw Gold

One of the most notorious outlaws to ever terrorize banks, railroads, and stagecoaches in Kansas and Oklahoma was Bill Doolin. Unlike many outlaws and robbers associated with the Wild West, Doolin never spent his loot on women, gambling, or drink. Instead, the near-legendary bandit was a devoted family man and, according to researchers, a miser. In spite of having netted more than $175,000 in robberies over the two-year period preceding his death, Doolin lived frugally and apparently buried the bulk of his fortune near a frame shack located in Burden, Kansas. Because Doolin was killed before he was able to retrieve this money, it still lies there today.

During the early part of the 1890s, the Doolin Gang was the most efficient and successful gang of robbers in eastern Oklahoma, southern Kansas, southwestern Missouri, and even parts of Texas.

During one extended spree of robberies, the gang netted $11,000 from the bank in Spearville, Kansas, and then rode to Cimarron, Kansas, two days later and robbed $14,000 from that town's bank. Doolin then led his outlaw band to Southwest City, Missouri, and stole $15,000 from its bank. On the way to one of their numerous hideouts in Oklahoma, they passed through the town of Pawnee where they robbed the city bank of several more thousands of dollars in gold coins. Following this, the bandits traveled to Longview, Texas, where they took just over $50,000 from a bank.

When they were not robbing banks, the Doolin Gang found stagecoaches and trains easy targets. Using dynamite to blast open the express cars, they held up three trains near Wharton, Oklahoma, and a railroad depot at Woodward.

While Bill Doolin was well-respected, even admired, by his gang members, he had a reputation of being very stingy when it came to dividing the loot, doling out small portions to his men while he kept the largest percentage for himself. When the other outlaws visited towns and spent freely on women and alcohol, Doolin preferred remaining in camp and counting his money.

While on a train robbery rampage in Kansas, Doolin discovered the small and somewhat isolated community of Burden located in Cowley County and about forty miles southeast of Wichita. There Doolin purchased a plot of land with a weathered frame house, and when he was not roaming the countryside robbing banks, trains, and stagecoaches, he retreated to this quiet place and lived in peace and reclusion. It was near this shack that Doolin buried his robbery loot.

In December 1895, Doolin retreated to Eureka Springs, Arkansas, a thriving resort town, to relax after a series of successful robberies. Though still a relatively young man, Doolin suffered from arthritis and often journeyed to this spa city to bathe in its mineral waters.

While peacefully soaking in a hot mineral bath, Doolin was surprised one afternoon by Deputy Marshall Bill Tilghman who leveled a pistol at the naked outlaw and placed him under arrest. A few days later, Doolin was locked in the Guthrie, Oklahoma, jail to await trial for bank robbery.

Doolin, realizing that if he ever went to trial he would be convicted and sent to prison, knew his only chance for freedom was to escape from the Guthrie jail. During his first week in the cell, Doolin made friends with the night guard. After a week in the jail, the outlaw told the jailer about the fortune in robbery loot he had buried in a secret location in Kansas. The guard, excited by the tales of great wealth that the outlaw would never get to spend, listened intently to Doolin's tales about gold coins and thick wads of currency.

Late one night, Doolin told the jailer that because he would probably never see his buried fortune again he had decided to give it away. He asked the guard to bring him a piece of paper and a pencil so he could draw a map to the location of the loot.

Excited, the guard abandoned all caution as he brought the requested items to the notorious bank robber. As he handed Doolin the paper and pencil, the outlaw grabbed the guard's arm and pulled him sharply up against the cell's iron bars. As he applied leverage to the arm of the surprised jailer, Doolin relieved him of his pistol and jail keys. Still holding onto the guard, the outlaw unlocked the cell door. After knocking the jailer unconscious, Doolin dragged him into the cell and locked him inside. After stealing a horse and buggy, Doolin rode away into the night and was not seen again for several weeks. Most believed the outlaw retreated to one of his many hideouts in the Osage Hills in eastern Oklahoma, but he actually fled to the seclusion of his secret place in Burden where he spent his days counting his money and making plans to retire from banditry, move his wife and child to Kansas, and begin a new life ranching and farming on the bounteous plains.

For days, posses of armed deputies combed the Oklahoma countryside looking for the outlaw but were unable to find any trace of him. Eventually, they all gave up the search and returned home.

All but one. Heck Thomas, a lawman, had gained fame during the preceding years for his tenacity in tracking bandits and bringing them to justice. Thomas was very familiar with Bill Doolin and his habits. He also knew that Doolin was a devoted family man who adored his wife and child. After asking some discrete questions while tracking the escapee through central Oklahoma, Thomas learned that the outlaw's wife and child were currently living with her father in Lawton, Oklahoma. Knowing that Doolin would eventually go to his family, Thomas waited patiently in Lawton and kept a close watch on Mrs. Doolin.

Thomas was not to be disappointed. Within two days after Thomas's arrival, Doolin rode the stolen horse and buggy right up to the front door of his father-in-law's house. After the outlaw went inside, Thomas hid behind a large tree and watched the house.

About two hours later, Doolin, his wife, and child came out of the house. After throwing several pieces of luggage in the back of the wagon, Doolin helped his family climb aboard and settle into the spring seat. At this point, Thomas came from behind the tree and approached the wagon. Doolin spotted the lawman before he had taken two steps and grabbed for a rifle that laid under the wagon seat. As he raised the weapon, Doolin was cut down with a single bullet from Thomas's gun. Before he hit the ground, one of the most notorious robbers that ever rode the southern Great Plains was dead.

Anyone who followed the outlaw career of Bill Doolin knew that he had hidden tens of thousands of dollars' worth of robbery loot. Most suspected it was cached in one or more of the many hide-outs in the eastern Oklahoma hills, but continuous searches over the succeeding years failed to locate the treasure.

Nearly twenty years following Bill Doolin's death, the identity of his secret hideaway in Burden, Kansas, was discovered. By the time treasure hunters arrived at the location, little was left of the weathered, tumbled-down house, and weeds and brush had reclaimed most of the yard. While some excavation of the property was undertaken, not a single coin from the fabulous Doolin cache was ever found.

Based on the available evidence, most researchers believe Doolin's treasure still lies buried somewhere at Burden. This tiny town of about five hundred residents is situated in rolling prairie and farmland, and a few of the older residents still relate stories they heard from their parents about Bill Doolin seeking refuge here. A few claim to know exactly where the old Doolin shack once stood, but all admit to some confusion when asked to identify the site.

Records of such things surely exist. Perhaps, some dusty courthouse documents contain information on the property once owned by Doolin who used an assumed name. Someone, perhaps, has an old journal that relates the outlaw's visits to the region. Someday, someone with luck and patience may discover important clues that will eventually lead them to Bill Doolin's buried cache of outlaw loot.

The Fate of the Chavez Gold

One day in the early spring of 1843, a caravan departed Santa Fe, New Mexico, bound for Westport, Missouri. Don Antonio Jose Chavez, a descendant of the powerful Chavez family who once governed this part of New Mexico, led the caravan. Chavez, a successful businessman and trader, was accompanied by five servants who herded fifty-five fine mules and drove two wagons laden with trade goods. After arriving at Westport, Chavez intended to sell the mules and goods for a huge profit. After remaining in Westport for a few days, he would return to Santa Fe in the company of his hired help. In one of the heavy wagons, Chavez transported a large wooden trunk filled with bolts of cloth. Known only to the trader, this trunk had a false bottom that was stuffed with approximately $12,000 in gold coins.

More than six hundred miles away in Westport, a desperate-looking man named Jack McDaniel mysteriously learned about Chavez's caravan. It was well-known among Westport businessmen that Chavez made such a trip at least once every year, and that he always brought along a fine herd of mules to sell. It was rumored that Chavez often carried large sums of money on his journeys and the Mexican trader traveled with only a small contingent of unarmed men. Therefore, he was susceptible to robbery. In Chavez, McDaniel saw an opportunity to make a quick profit.

Though he sometimes identified himself as a military officer and other times as a scout, McDaniel, accompanied by a band of a dozen hard-edged drifters and outlaws, earned his living preying on unwary travelers along the Santa Fe Trail. When McDaniel learned of Chavez's departure from Santa Fe, he assembled his men and left Westport in the middle of the night, intending to encounter the Mexican somewhere along the trail and help himself to his money and mules.

Chavez's journey was fraught with mishap from the start. Caught in a sudden and unexpected late season snowstorm in western Kansas, he lost fifty mules when they died in the bitter cold and raging wind. When the blizzard finally passed and the skies cleared, one of the wagons, along with its entire contents, was lost while crossing the flood-swollen Arkansas River. With only the trunk full of gold, five mules, and a pitifully small selection of trade goods, Chavez and his men continued on toward Westport.

Sometime during the second week of April, the Chavez party arrived at Cow Creek Crossing just west of present-day Lyons in Rice County, about thirty-five miles east of Great Bend. Chavez decided to stop there for a few days and give his men and livestock some needed rest before proceeding on to Westport. The trader located a suitable site in a grove of trees not far from one of the many dry ravines that cut criss-cross patterns throughout this region.

On the evening of the second day at this location as Chavez's servants were preparing dinner, a band of riders appeared on the horizon, apparently heading toward the camp. Initially supposing these newcomers to be Indians, the Mexicans readied their few poor rifles in anticipation of an attack, but as the riders neared, the campers believed them to be nothing more than weary travelers and invited them to dismount and share dinner.

As Jack McDaniel and the twelve newcomers rode into the camp, they were dismayed by the caravan's small size. Seeing only one wagon and five mules, McDaniel initially concluded this couldn't be the Chavez party. More irritated than anything else, the outlaw led his band into the camp.

As Chavez rose to greet the newcomers, McDaniel and his henchmen pointed their rifles and pistols at the unsuspecting Mexicans. While one of the bandits went to look over the five remaining mules, McDaniel and another man jumped into the wagon and began searching through it. Prying the lid off the large wooden trunk, McDaniel removed bolts of cloth, tossing them out of the wagon and into the dirt. After emptying the trunk, McDaniel's companion informed him nothing else was in the wagon save for a few useless trade items. Growing angry, McDaniel leaped to the ground and approached the Mexican trader. Grabbing him by his coat lapels, the outlaw shook Chavez violently, screaming at him and insisting he turn over his gold immediately. Chavez's only response was silence. Frustrated, McDaniel pulled a pistol from his belt and knocked the Mexican unconscious. Turning to his companions, he ordered them to search the camp thoroughly.

Finding nothing, McDaniel assembled all the servants, along with Chavez, in the center of the camp. As the fire burned low and cast flickering shadows across the faces of the frightened Mexicans, McDaniel demanded the gold be turned over to him or he would kill one of them. The servants, knowing nothing about the gold Chavez had hidden in the trunk, merely stared in terror at the fierce bandits. Chavez, believing the outlaws would soon grow discouraged and leave, refused to reveal the existence of the false trunk bottom.

After Chavez refused several requests to turn his gold over to the bandits, McDaniel walked up to him, placed the tip of his pistol barrel against the trader's ear, and blew his head off.

After chasing the servants away, the outlaws tossed all of the camp equipment and trade goods onto the fire. As it was blazing brightly, McDaniel grabbed a burning brand from the pile and threw it into the wagon bed. A few minutes later after the wagon erupted in flames, the outlaws pushed it into the nearby ravine, watching it break into fiery pieces when it struck bottom. The scattered planks continued to burn, illuminating the walls of the deep, narrow gully.

The next morning when the bandits rode away from the campground, they departed with no knowledge whatsoever of the fortune in gold coins that lie among the smoldering ruins of the wagon at the ravine's bottom.

Three days later while returning to Westport, the McDaniel Gang was approached by a platoon of mounted soldiers. Assuming the cavalrymen were pursuing them, McDaniel and his men fired at them and a fierce gun battle ensued. When it was over, several outlaws and soldiers were dead and McDaniel, along with a companion named DePrefontaine, was captured. After a short trial, DePrefontaine was sentenced to prison but was later granted a pardon. McDaniel was eventually hung.

Months later, after learning of the fate of Chavez, several of his relatives made the long journey to Cow Creek Crossing in a vain effort to recover his body and locate the missing fortune in gold coins. They failed at both objectives.

Somewhere, mixed in with the sands and gravel that comprise the bottom of one of the several ravines found near Cow Creek Crossing not far from the present-day town of Lyons, Kansas, lies a great fortune of gold coins, each stamped with an early nineteenth century mint date. Though runoff from thousands of thunderstorms have flowed through the ravine since the burning wagon was rolled into it, the gold, one of the world's heavier metals, would not have been carried away. Instead, it likely sank through the top layer of lighter, finer sands and eventually came to rest a few inches below, perhaps lodged on a layer of bedrock.

There it lies today, still unclaimed, still undiscovered after a century and a half.

Nebraska

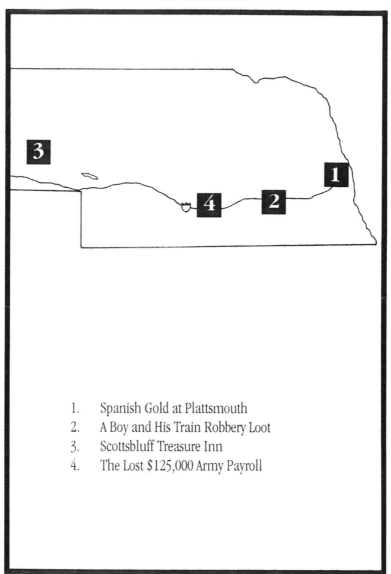

1. Spanish Gold at Plattsmouth
2. A Boy and His Train Robbery Loot
3. Scottsbluff Treasure Inn
4. The Lost $125,000 Army Payroll

Spanish Gold at Plattsmouth

During the late 1850s, Plattsmouth, Nebraska, was an important town located near a major crossing on the Missouri River. Important, because it was the last place gold-seekers traveling westward could get outfitted and purchase supplies before entering the mountains.

As the gold rush of the mid-nineteenth century lured hopeful men from the east and south, Plattsmouth prospered better than any other Nebraska town, and during that time its future looked brighter than Omaha, located some twenty miles to the north.

From the time gold was discovered near Denver, Colorado, in 1858, a steady stream of men, each believing he would strike it rich in the Rockies, passed through Plattsmouth on their way to the gold fields. Because it was the last town of any size before reaching the Rocky Mountains, the eager, profit-minded merchants charged premium prices for the tools, supplies, and riding stock needed by the enthusiastic prospectors. The merchants claimed extensive knowledge of gold mining in the west, raised the hopes of the miners, and often sold the naive new arrivals considerably more than they needed and at higher than normal prices. The gold seekers spent a great deal of money in the town before continuing on their westward trek.

Many Plattsmouth merchants and city officials even encouraged the miners to return to the town, settle down, and claim a piece of land after finding their fortunes in Colorado. Many did, because very few of the thousands that trekked westward across mid-America and the Great Plains ever found gold in significant quantities. Most of the miners were barely able to scrape by, thousands went broke, and many quit the area and returned east after only a few weeks in the rugged mountains.

As they traveled eastward after abandoning the failed diggings and the empty shafts, it was the practice of many travelers during those times to bury what gold and money they possessed when they stopped for the night. If, perchance, they were visited by robbers, they could turn out their pockets and convince the would-be thieves they had no money. Many prospectors and miners who left Colorado, while not striking it rich, were able to hoard some small amount of gold that they brought back with them, and at each stop they buried it near their campsite.

Many of those who quit the mines and the streams in the Rockies often encountered large parties of eager and hopeful gold seekers heading westward along the trail. The newcomers were always disheartened to hear the hard luck stories related by the unsuccessful miners, and many turned back at that point.

During the spring of 1859, a group of nearly one hundred unlucky prospectors, after several weeks of weary traveling, was approaching Plattsmouth from the west one evening when they decided to stop and camp for the night on a low rise located about two miles from the town. As was custom, a hole was excavated, and in turn each traveler deposited his marked leather pouches containing gold dust, nuggets, and coins. While not a single one of the group possessed what could be considered a fortune, the combined total of the buried gold amounted to several thousand dollars.

As the group of unlucky miners went about the business of setting up camp, a westbound party consisting of about two hundred men, all inexperienced but enthusiastic gold seekers, approached from the direction of Plattsmouth. All had purchased expensive supplies in the town earlier that day and their eagerness to get to Colorado and dig for gold was clearly manifested in their countenances and demeanor. The party rode up to the campsite of the returning miners who, in turn, invited the travelers to join them for the evening.

During subsequent discussions around several campfires that night, the experienced prospectors pointed out to the newcomers how much of their recently purchased equipment was useless in the mountains and how the merchants and shopkeepers in town had tricked all of them into making unnecessary purchases. The more the prospectors spoke about being cheated by the Plattsmouth merchants, the angrier they became. The miners also informed the immigrants that gold was not as easy to find as the town's storekeepers led them to believe. Eventually, tempers rose and the two groups of men decided to band together, storm into the town, and loot it in order to exact revenge on the merchants and reclaim some of their expenses.

One of the westbound hopefuls observed the growing resentment of the miners toward the townsfolk and grew concerned about the possibility of innocent people getting hurt. So he quietly slipped away from the campsite and rode to Plattsmouth to warn the residents.

Within the hour, an angry horde of vengeful men stormed toward Plattsmouth. Many were armed with pistols and rifles and a few carried clubs and knives. All of their wagons, livestock, supplies, and gold remained at the campsite west of town.

Thanks to the warning they received earlier in the evening, Plattsmouth residents were well-prepared for the attacking force. Hundreds of armed citizens took positions at the edge of town and along the road where the angry men approached.

As the mob arrived on the outskirts of the city, they were met by the band of citizens who commanded them to drop their weapons. Clearly outnumbered, the would-be invaders meekly surrendered. Embarrassed at being so quickly and efficiently subdued, the group was then herded together and marched through town toward the Missouri River. On reaching the west bank of the wide river, they were ordered by the defenders to swim across to Iowa or be shot where they stood. To emphasize their demands, several townspeople fired shots over the heads of the prisoners.

Dozens of men immediately jumped into the river and swam to the other side. Many who couldn't swim pleaded for mercy from the citizens but were promptly thrown pieces of driftwood on which to float across. Within thirty minutes, the entire group of three hundred men stood on the Iowa side of the river. They were cold, wet, and angry, and as they shivered in the cool of the evening, they lined the opposite bank shaking their fists and shouting curses and threats at the armed townsfolk who merely turned away and walked home.

The next morning, dozens of the town's citizens rose early and rode on horseback and drove wagons out to the recently abandoned campsite west of town. They helped themselves to the abandoned goods, many of which were purchased in town only the day before. Wagons were taken and horses and oxen were procured. Even boots, cooking utensils, and camping gear that had been left were quickly grabbed up.

Unknown to the pillagers, however, the large cache of gold coins, nuggets, and dust was buried somewhere near the middle of the campsite. By noon, nothing remained in the area save for the ashes from the previous evening's fires.

Several years passed, and one day two travelers showed up at Plattsmouth—a pair of middle-aged men who had just crossed the Missouri River on a ferry. For three days they searched the area west of the town near the road for the old campsite but were never able to relocate it. Years of rain, erosion, and farming had changed the character and shape of the landscape in that region. Discouraged, they returned to the town where they told several citizens that, as young men, they were among the group that was chased out of town and across the river in 1859. They related that the miners had buried a fortune in gold in a shallow hole near the middle of the camp and that they had returned to try to recover it.

To the relief and delight of the newcomers, the residents harbored no grudges against them, and several even volunteered to help them locate the old campground. Many of the old-timers who aided in the search were among those who participated in chasing the miners out of town years earlier. Several of them claimed to recall the old campsite's exact location, but after accompanying the two strangers to the area, it was clear that the passing years had dimmed their memories, for it was never found.

The gold carried by the returning miners in 1859 continues to lay beneath the sod of the plains on a low rise of ground just west of Plattsmouth, now a healthy community of about six thousand five hundred citizens. Today, the value of the gold would be nearly twenty-five times what it was when it was buried. The coins would also carry tremendous values as collectors' items.

It is entirely possible that if anyone could ever locate the exact site of the miners' campsite, a great fortune in buried gold could be recovered with some patience, persistence, and a good metal detector.

A Boy and His Train Robbery Loot

Duke Sherman was tired. He was tired of mucking out the feedlots and stables at the Omaha stockyards. He was tired of never having enough money to go into town to drink and gamble with his friends. He was tired of being bossed around by the yardmaster. Duke Sherman was tired of his life, and he was determined to change it before he became resigned to a life of sweeping manure and taking orders from others.

A year earlier, the seventeen-year-old Sherman left the Iowa farm where he was raised to sample life in the big city. Arriving in Omaha, the youth used up the small amount of money he carried in two days and was forced to seek work at the stockyards. From time to time, he attempted to hire out on one of the wagon trains heading west, but the older, more experienced riders always won the positions. Believing he was so far down on his luck that he couldn't get any lower, Duke Sherman decided to rob a train.

One evening while hanging around the train depot, Sherman overheard a conversation between the telegrapher and Ed Walz, an engineer. Walz was telling his friend about a shipment of gold leaving on the morning express run bound for Lincoln, about fifty miles to the southwest. The shipment, valued at $60,000, was to be delivered to a bank in Lincoln that would use it to invest in property for the railroad. The gold would be transported in the messenger car in several metal boxes.

Sixty thousand dollars! Sherman thought to himself. If he could get his hands on that kind of money, he would no longer have to sweep out cattle pens and stables. Seizing on an idea, Sherman returned to the stockyards, stole a horse and buckboard, and rode all night alongside the railroad tracks that led to Lincoln.

Around mid-morning of the next day, Walz spotted a herd of cattle milling about on the tracks about ten miles out of Lincoln. Slowing the train, he blew the whistle hoping to frighten the bovines from the locomotive's path. As the cattle slowly dispersed, Walz dropped the speed to just under ten miles per hour. As he was about to yank the whistle cord once again, he felt a sharp jab in his ribs. Turning, he looked into a face, covered in a red checkered bandanna, of a man holding him at gunpoint. On the other side of the masked man, Walz spotted his unconscious assistant lying on the floor of the cab, his head bleeding from a severe blow.

Duke Sherman ordered Walz to stop the train. Walz, stunned by the sudden and frightening circumstances, only stood stiff and still and gaped at the newcomer. An instant later, Sherman cracked the engineer on the side of the head with his pistol, knocking him to the floor. Pulling Walz to his feet, Sherman once again told him to stop the train, which he did immediately.

At gunpoint, Sherman then led the stunned and bleeding engineer to the messenger car. When the train halted a few moments earlier, the messenger had opened the door and was peering out when Sherman and the engineer arrived. Sherman informed the messenger that if he didn't throw the metal boxes of gold coins on the ground next to the tracks he would kill the engineer. The frightened messenger paused only a second before obeying the order, and within minutes the $60,000 laid on the ground beside the train.

Sherman then led Walz back to the engine and told him to climb in and take the train on to Lincoln. As the locomotive pulled away, Walz looked out of the cab and saw the robber drive a buckboard from behind a nearby grove of trees toward the gold. As the train turned a bend and Walz lost sight of the bandit, Sherman was busily loading the heavy boxes onto the bed of the wagon. Moments later, the outlaw was whipping the single horse-drawn wagon across the open prairie and toward the northwest, toward Central City where he intended to hide his new fortune and make plans to start a new life.

Like many youths who decide to turn to crime, Sherman lacked the skills and experience for thorough planning and execution. While stealing the horse and wagon in Omaha, he was seen and recognized by at least three people. As he was riding away from the stockyards, the town marshal was awakened and informed of the theft. Before dawn, a posse of a dozen deputized citizens set out in search of the youth.

Sherman also failed to consider the weight of the gold. Sixty thousand dollars in gold coins represented a significant load for the small wagon and was difficult for the single horse to pull efficiently, and by the time ten miles were covered at a run, the horse began to feel the strain.

After crossing the Big Blue River near the present-day town of Staplehurst, the horse grew lame and was slowed to a limping walk. After another two miles, it stopped altogether.

Sherman cursed the horse and considered shooting it when his anger finally subsided. Desperate to transport his new wealth to Central City, he needed to obtain a healthy horse to pull the wagon. Since this was ranching country, he decided it would be a simple task to steal one, attach it to the wagon, and be on his way. He unhitched the injured animal and turned it loose to graze on the prairie grasses.

As Sherman pondered the direction to take in search of a farm or ranch, he considered the gold in the back of the wagon. It would be foolish, he thought, to leave it out in the open where a passing horseman might find it. One by one, Sherman unloaded the boxes and buried them in a shallow excavation about twenty yards from the wagon. After filling the hole, he covered it with grass, making it look like the rest of the prairie. Realizing the lone wagon sitting in the middle of the open plain would be easy to spot from a long way off, he set out in search of a fresh horse.

Two hours after Sherman abandoned the wagon, the posse that had been following its tracks came upon it. After learning of the train robbery earlier, they found the place where the gold-filled boxes were unloaded and easily tracked the heavily laden wagon to this location. On arriving, however, the marshal was puzzled by the absence of the horse and the outlaw.

A few minutes later, one of the deputies found the crippled horse, led it back to the wagon, and suggested the outlaw was probably forced to search for a new one. Another deputy offered that the robber probably buried the gold someplace between the robbery site and the wagon.

The marshal split the posse into two groups, half going off to look for the train robber, and the other half backtracking along the trail in search of a place where the gold might have been cached. After hitching the wagon to his horse, another of the deputies climbed aboard, turned the vehicle around, and followed his companions back down the trail. Just behind the departing posse, a vast number of gold coins laid mere inches below the surface.

The group of men who followed Sherman's trail back to the railroad tracks found no sign of the gold and finally returned to Omaha.

Around mid-morning on the next day, a farmer surprised Duke Sherman in his barn as the youth was placing a bridle on one of the horses. Startled by the farmer, Sherman pulled his pistol and shot him, wounding him in the shoulder. The farmer turned, ran to his house, and retrieved a shotgun. As the young outlaw rode the stolen horse bareback out of the barn, the farmer raced out onto his front porch and blasted Sherman off the mount with two loads of buckshot.

As he lay dying in the farmer's yard, Sherman tried to explain about the gold buried near the wagon, but the farmer understood little of what he said.

Duke Sherman never lived to realize his dream of wealth and was buried in some lonely spot out on the prairie. To this day, the $60,000 in gold coins, worth many times that amount now, still lies in some unknown location not far from Staplehurst.

Scottsbluff Treasure Inn

The period of westward migration in the United States saw thousands of hopeful citizens traveling across the Great Plains in search of land and opportunity. As more and more migrants journeyed to California, Washington, Oregon, the Rocky Mountains, and to the western edges of some of the plains states, several major trails became established along which small towns sprang up to serve the traveler's needs.

Scottsbluff, Nebraska, was a town where migrants could rest themselves and their draft animals for several days and replenish supplies before continuing their long westward trek. Mercantiles and liveries did a brisk business, as did saloons and gambling halls.

Many of the more prosperous travelers made the trip west by coach and, on arriving at the various towns that dotted the prairie along the route, would spend the night at a hotel. As a result, many fine taverns, fashionable hotels, and plush inns were established in places such as Omaha, Grand Island, North Platte, and Scottsbluff.

One day a man named Bolton arrived at Scottsbluff from the east. Bolton was obviously a man of means and went about town dressed in a waistcoat and top hat and flashed an expensive pocket watch. He was a quiet man, almost surly, and for the most part he shunned the company of others save for the few with whom he conducted business. Thick of brow, beady of eye, and heavy of bone, Bolton possessed a sinister look and rough demeanor. No one in Scottsbluff knew anything about his past, but it was rumored he was chased from some large eastern city because he was suspected of involvement in several bizarre killings.

Within a few months after arriving in this western Nebraska town, Bolton purchased some land and supervised the construction of a large hotel, which he believed would prove attractive to the growing numbers of moneyed travelers who perceived grand business opportunities in the west.

When the hotel was completed, it offered exquisite, well-furnished rooms, a huge, carved wood bar imported from Philadelphia, and a spacious restaurant that served juicy steaks, fresh oysters and venison, imported wines, and expensive liquors.

Bolton was a shrewd businessman but an inept and luckless gambler. His uncontrolled passion for cards and dice kept him occupied most nights, but his lack of skill caused him to lose several thousand dollars on many occasions. Though Bolton's hotel and restaurant thrived, his gambling debts drove him to the point of near bankruptcy. Frustrated and fearful, he grew desperate and cast about for ways to come into some money to support his hotel.

One evening, Bolton watched a man drinking alone at one of the tables in the restaurant. It was obvious this was a man of means from the fine clothes he wore and the expensive rings that adorned his fingers. When the man paid for his drinks, Bolton noted that he pulled gold coins from a tooled-leather pouch attached to his belt. After observing the customer for several minutes, Bolton had an idea and approached the man.

After introducing himself to the customer, Bolton told him that he perceived him as a man of discerning tastes and invited him to accompany him to the wine cellar and help select some dinner wines. Pleased at the invitation, the customer rose and followed Bolton to the rear of the building and down a steep ladder into the cellar.

As the customer perused the racks filled with fine imported wines, Bolton attacked him from behind and snapped his neck with his big, meaty hands, killing him instantly. Quickly, Bolton removed the victim's leather pouch and counted well over $2,000 in gold coins. Locating a shovel in a far corner of the cellar, Bolton excavated a shallow grave, laid the body into it, and covered it over. Never, the hotel owner thought to himself, had making money been so easy.

During the next three months, several newcomers to Scottsbluff mysteriously disappeared. All were men of some wealth, and all were last seen in Bolton's establishment. Though Bolton was questioned on several occasions by law enforcement officials, he was never suspected of being involved in any of the disappearances.

In time, Bolton paid off his gambling debts and vowed never to indulge again in games of chance. Instead, Bolton became addicted to killing and to the ease and neatness of removing large amounts of gold and silver coins and currency from his unlucky victims. Not only had Bolton become obsessed with killing, he became passionate about hoarding his new wealth. Over the next few years, the strange hotel owner grew more miserly and reclusive.

Bolton gradually came to distrust banks and soon closed his accounts in town. As he accumulated a fortune in gold coins, currency, and jewelry from his murdered victims, he developed the habit of burying the loot in the cellar in the corner opposite from where he interred his victims. After several years, the entire wine cellar had been dug up to accommodate Bolton's wealth and the grisly remains of the dead.

Bolton's undoing was attributed to the careless manner in which he disposed of the horses belonging to his victims. Because the murdered men often tied their horses out in front of his hotel before entering, Bolton learned early to move them to another location so they would not cast suspicion in his direction. Occasionally, he tied the horses in front of a saloon in another part of town, but he eventually discovered that good horses brought a good price on the open market and he began selling them.

Most of the time, Bolton accumulated several mounts and herded them eastward to North Platte where he sold them. Unfortunately, a horse belonging to one of his victims was spotted in that town and traced back to the hotel owner. Soon, North Platte and Scottsbluff law enforcement officials began comparing notes and decided Bolton was somehow linked to the missing men.

When the town marshal insisted on searching Bolton's hotel, the proprietor happily escorted him around. While inspecting the wine cellar, the marshal saw nothing out of the ordinary and, perplexed, concluded his search.

Rumors of Bolton's potential involvement in the murders began to spread through town and soon the citizens talked openly about their own suspicions of the hotel owner. As the weeks passed, more and more travelers heard the stories of men disappearing in the hotel and refused to stay there. Eventually, Bolton closed the hotel and had it boarded up.

Meanwhile, the town marshal decided to search the hotel premises one more time and deputized several citizens to help him. This time, however, Bolton refused to allow them inside and threatened to fire upon the intruders if they persisted. Enraged, Scottsbluff citizens voiced their concerns to the marshal, claiming if he did not do something about Bolton they would take matters into their own hands.

About an hour before dawn of the following day, a group of five Scottsbluff citizens quietly crept to the rear of Bolton's hotel, splashed several buckets of coal oil onto the walls, and set the place afire. As the building burned, Bolton could be heard screaming and firing his rifle inside, but as the roaring inferno completely engulfed the wooden structure, his voice faded.

For several weeks after Bolton's death and the hotel fire, area residents stopped to gaze at the pile of ashes and charred timbers. Little did they know that a fortune in gold coins, currency, and jewelry lay buried in the former wine cellar, now completely filled in and covered by the debris.

Several years later, a man named Bennett purchased the land where Bolton's hotel once stood. During the process of removing the charred debris from the lot, one of Bennett's workers happened to be throwing old timbers from what apparently was once a wine cellar. Reaching down to seize one such timber, the worker was startled to see a human bone protruding from the dirt floor. He informed Bennett, and the businessman hastened to investigate.

After several more skeletons were dug up, Bennett assumed this was where the infamous Bolton buried his victims years earlier. Completely unaware of the huge fortune buried only a few feet from the dead men's bones, Bennett instructed his workers to rebury the skeletons and fill in the old wine cellar.

Today, no one is entirely certain of the exact site where Bolton's hotel was located. Since that time, Scottsbluff has evolved into an important city on the Great Plains and has changed dramatically.

It has been estimated that Bolton may have buried as much as $100,000 in stolen coins and currency, an amount that would conservatively be worth over a $500,000 today.

The Bolton treasure has never been recovered and remains buried near his many victims' skeletons in the bottom of that long-forgotten wine cellar.

The Lost $125,000 Army Payroll

As more and more settlers arrived in the Great Plains soon after the Civil War, the need for protection and law enforcement grew. Between the late 1860s and the mid-1890s, thousands of these migrants, who perceived grand agricultural opportunities on the vast Great Plains, as well as scores of merchants who kept farmers supplied with equipment, continuously petitioned the federal government for increased and better protection from marauding Indians and growing numbers of outlaws.

In response, the United States government ordered the establishment of a chain of military forts and temporary outpost garrisons throughout much of the Great Plains. Thousands of troopers were stationed throughout the region with orders to protect the citizens. Wherever large numbers of soldiers were found, huge payrolls soon followed, and the subsequent transportation of gold specie and currency into these remote regions became common.

For years, the delivery of such payrolls to scattered outposts was difficult and soldiers often waited for months without pay. As the military tried to meet payment schedules, wagons carrying large payrolls and following assigned schedules often departed St. Louis or Kansas City, Missouri, bound for the hinterlands. These payroll wagons were always accompanied by an armed military escort and often spent weeks on the long and lonely trail before arriving at a selected destination.

On a sweltering July afternoon in 1874, a plank-sided payroll wagon pulled by a team of four sturdy horses and accompanied by a platoon of twelve armed cavalrymen plied the rugged route from Kansas City, Missouri, to Fort Kearney, located on the Platte River in south-central Nebraska. Since departing Kansas City twelve days earlier, the wagon and escort struggled through a series of severe rainstorms, which washed out the already poor roads and at times caused the party to stop altogether for hours at a time. Driven by veteran teamster Hollis Brown, the durable wooden wagon with large, steel rimmed wheels, carried $125,000 in gold coins—payroll for the troops stationed at Fort Kearney.

Because bandits often stalked the trails linking major towns in the region, the escort was ever watchful and extremely cautious during the journey's early phase. As the days wore on and fewer and fewer travelers were encountered along the route, however, the escort began to relax its guard, and the detachment of once stern-visaged and alert soldiers had degenerated into an undisciplined, carefree, jocular band of unconcerned cavalrymen. Even Lieutenant Lewis Pendergrast, the escort's commanding officer, grew bored with the assignment and permitted his charges to purchase alcohol, which they commenced drinking around mid-morning each day, in the small settlements along the route.

When Hollis Brown first took the reins of the payroll wagon in Kansas City, he had a bad feeling about this particular escort. A veteran of dozens of trips into and across the Great Plains, Brown was very knowledgeable about the potential dangers of the Sioux who roamed this region. On more than one occasion, Brown had been chased by Indians, and while transporting a payroll the previous year, his wagon had been attacked by a band of highwaymen intent on stealing its rich cargo. During the subsequent flight across the prairie, the driver's partner was shot and killed but Brown, although he received a severe shoulder wound, managed to save the payroll. On this sweltering day, he rubbed the growing, throbbing pain in his shoulder, an ever-present reminder of the danger on these plains, and steered the wagon along its course. He regarded the ineffective escort riding about thirty yards to the rear of the wagon.

Hollis Brown was not impressed with Lieutenant Pendergrast and his escort. He considered the officer immature, cowardly, and careless to the point of being derelict in his duties. Brown made a mental note to report the young lieutenant to authorities upon arrival at Fort Kearney. Brown and his co-driver, Alexander Hamilton, tired of the soldiers' drinking and gambling in the evenings, chose to bed down some distance away.

As Brown kept the horses at a consistent walk, gradually covering the miles of seemingly endless prairie, he searched the countryside for a suitable location to stop and provide a short break for animals and men alike. As he scanned the horizon, Brown spotted a dozen men riding up out of a nearby ravine and advancing toward the wagon at a brisk trot. Each of the men carried a carbine.

Brown immediately yelled a warning to the escort behind him. The troopers were laughing loudly and passing a bottle and did not hear the driver. Disgusted with the soldiers and realizing they would be useless in a fight, Brown told Hamilton to prepare to defend the payroll as he lashed the horses into a furious gallop.

As the payroll wagon sped down the trail, four of the oncoming riders split from the group and pursued the wagon. The remaining intruders positioned themselves between the fleeing wagon and the troopers and began firing into their midst. Brown could hear the shooting behind him and, on stealing a quick glance to the rear, saw most of the unprepared and surprised soldiers being shot from their horses.

The four riders in pursuit of the wagon were rapidly gaining on the heavy, somewhat cumbersome, vehicle. When they were within thirty yards, Hamilton fired, each of his first two shots knocking a rider out of the saddle. Impressed with Hamilton's marksmanship, the remaining two slowed their pace, staying approximately sixty yards away and waiting for their companions to catch up.

After six miles of maintaining a strong pace, the horses pulling the wagon showed signs of fatigue, and Brown slowed them to a trot. As he searched the prairie for some kind of shelter, Hamilton informed him the two riders had been joined by six more, apparently the survivors of the skirmish with the soldiers.

Moments later, Brown spotted a buffalo wallow a short distance to the south of the trail. He whipped the tired horses into a mad dash to reach the wallow before the riders could discern his intention and try to overtake the wagon. As the outlaws fired in the wagon's direction, Brown guided the vehicle into the lowest part of the wallow and set the brake. The two men leapt to the ground and took positions on the sheltered side of the low bank that faced the oncoming highwaymen. Hamilton aimed his rifle toward the advancing gang while Brown readied a revolver that he retrieved from beneath the wagon seat.

Believing the drivers were hopelessly trapped, the outlaws casually rode toward the wallow. When they were within forty yards, Hamilton rose up and killed two of them with as many shots. Brown likewise fired into the group but managed only to wound two of their horses.

Startled by the sudden attack, the bandits milled about for a few seconds before retreating a safe distance. When the outlaws were out of sight, Hamilton turned toward the wagon and noticed one of the lead horses had been killed and had fallen in its traces. Quickly, he cut the remaining horses loose and let them run onto the prairie.

After a tense hour of watching the horizon for the return of the outlaws, Brown spotted one of them approaching the buffalo wallow from the south. He turned to warn Hamilton and saw his partner pointing toward three more men coming in at a gallop from the north. Quickly scanning the prairie, the two desperate men spotted the others: one coming in from the west, the other riding hard from the east. A moment later, the bandits opened fire, hoping to overwhelm the men and take the gold payroll.

Hamilton killed two outlaws approaching from the north before he was slain with a bullet through his forehead. Brown grabbed his fallen partner's rifle and began firing wildly at the attackers, killing two more before being struck in the thigh by a bullet and knocked to the ground.

With the rifle out of ammunition, Brown pulled his pistol from his belt and, from a kneeling position, prepared to fight to the last. As he clumsily tied a bandanna around his bleeding leg, the thunder of hooves to his rear alerted him to the approach of the two remaining riders as they spurred their horses over the rim of the wallow and bore down on his position. A shot from one of the outlaws struck Brown in the left forearm and shattered a bone. Reflexively, Brown fired back, striking one attacker square in the chest. A second later he was trampled by the horse ridden by the surviving outlaw and suffered several broken ribs.

Reining his mount around for another run at the wounded driver, the remaining outlaw charged Brown once again. In great pain, Brown rose to a standing position and, though his vision was clouded and he could barely see, he raised his pistol and fired at the oncoming bandit. The rider, firing his revolver, struck Brown twice more before falling from the saddle with a bullet through his heart.

With the air filled with gun smoke, Brown collapsed to the ground, unconscious before his head even struck the sandy bottom.

Hollis Brown woke suddenly, aware of an uncomfortable and unaccustomed weight on his chest. Rubbing caked dust from his eyes, he watched as a vulture hopped away from where he lay and over to a bloody carcass about fifteen feet away.

As Brown rolled over, the sudden pain that shot through his body reminded him of the several wounds he had received in the gunfight with the outlaws. As he lay in the dirt fighting off the urge to scream out in agony, he wondered why he was still alive.

Two more hours passed, and finally the bleeding and broken driver managed to rise to a standing position. All about him was carnage—dead men and horses. At least twenty vultures tore flesh from the bodies. Somehow, Brown realized, he had managed to kill the last of the attackers just before losing consciousness.

The strain of standing upright for only a few minutes began to take a toll on Brown, who had lost a great deal of blood. A wave of sickness surged up from deep within his stomach and his vision clouded over. He felt his knees begin to buckle, and just before he crumpled to the ground, he saw the payroll wagon just a few feet away, three buzzards feasting on the dead horse still tied in the traces.

Three days following the attack on the payroll wagon, Henry Taylor struggled to coax some speed out of the single, aged ox pulling a wagon down the rutted road toward the town of Hastings. The wagon was loaded down with household goods and his wife and three daughters. Very slowly, the wagon approached the outskirts of Hastings. Taylor, a Calvinist minister, claimed loudly and often that the Lord visited him one evening months earlier in Virginia and commanded him to travel west and deliver God's word to the Anglo heathens newly populating this vast and untamed grassland. Taylor took such things very seriously, in-formed his family of his mission, packed all their belongings, and struck out for some unknown destination. When Hastings was spotted in the distance, Taylor decided that it must be the chosen place, where he was to settle, build a church, and fulfill his destiny.

As Taylor initiated a tuneless rendition of a popular hymn, one of his daughters screamed and pointed to an object lying in the grass just off the trail. It took the minister a full minute to halt the ox, and after setting the brake, he climbed gingerly from the wagon seat and cautiously crept through the grass to where the body lay.

As Reverend Taylor leaned close to the body lying in the grass, Hollis Brown rolled over, groaned in pain, and spit a cupful of blood onto the ground. Moments later, the delirious man was riding in the back of the wagon bound toward Hastings, tended by the Taylor women.

A week later when Hollis Brown was able to sit up, he told his story—the attack on the payroll wagon, the killing of the military escort, and the subsequent fight in the buffalo wallow. Though he insisted he needed to travel to Fort Kearney to report the incident, he was unable to stand for more than a few minutes at a time.

In the days that followed, Brown told his story several times. Three Hastings residents left early one morning in search of the buffalo wallow containing the payroll wagon, but once out on the prairie, they found dozens of wallows, all looking exactly alike—bare. In Brown's semiconscious delirium, he was completely un-aware of the direction he crawled when he left the wallow.

Several days later, Hollis Brown died from his wounds and was buried in the Hastings cemetery.

There is no record to indicate that the U.S. Army ever made an attempt to recover the payroll wagon. Many who heard the amazing story of Hollis Brown and the abandonment of the gold in the buffalo wallow tried to find the fortune, but none were successful.

Years passed, and the story of the lost military payroll in some remote buffalo wallow on the Nebraska prairie was forgotten save for a few references in journals kept by residents of Hastings.

In 1970, Dan Conway, a Clint, Texas, cotton farmer and nationally-ranked skeet shooter, journeyed to the Nebraska plains to hunt pheasant with friends.

During a hunt in the Adams County prairie, Conway became separated from his companions and found himself about a half-mile west of the main group. A cold wind began blowing out of the north and, clad in only a light jacket, Conway sought shelter until his friends could join him. He soon came across an old buffalo wallow into which he descended and sat down in the shelter of a bank.

As Conway sat smoking a cigarette and listening to the prairie sounds, he spotted an object sticking out of the ground near the center of the wallow. Curious, he lay down his shotgun, walked over to it, and discovered it was a portion of a large, steel-rimmed wagon wheel. With nothing better to do, he dug into the wallow, eventually freeing the large wheel.

Moments later, his companions arrived. They left the wallow and returned to their vehicles parked about a mile away. Happy with his discovery, Conway rolled the large wheel ahead of him, intending to take it back to Texas.

Two nights later, as the pheasant hunters sat around a blazing hearth in their rented cabin, they were joined by a half-dozen visitors from nearby Hastings. One of the newcomers spied the wagon wheel and inquired about it. When Conway explained he had found it in an old buffalo wallow, the visitor grew quite excited and related a story about a lost military payroll told to him years earlier by his grandfather, the Reverend Henry Taylor. During the passage of so many years, the wagon, suggested Taylor's grandson, must have rotted away, dropping the gold shipment onto the ground where it was covered by subsequent deposition of wind-blown sand.

When the visitor finished the story, the group determined to return to the wallow the next morning with shovels and search for the gold. The next morning miles of prairie were searched, but the wallow from which Conway dug the wheel could not be found.

While writing this chapter, the author learned of a renewed attempt to locate the lost military payroll believed to be under a few inches of topsoil in the middle of a Nebraska buffalo wallow. A California physician learned about the treasure in 1988 and grew obsessed with the prospect of recovering it. The doctor, who owns two small airplanes and some remote sensing equipment, plans to conduct a series of low-level flights across the Nebraska prairie over Adams County in the hope that his detection equipment can locate the remains of the payroll wagon and the lost gold.

At today's values, the gold will likely be worth several million dollars.

NORTH DAKOTA

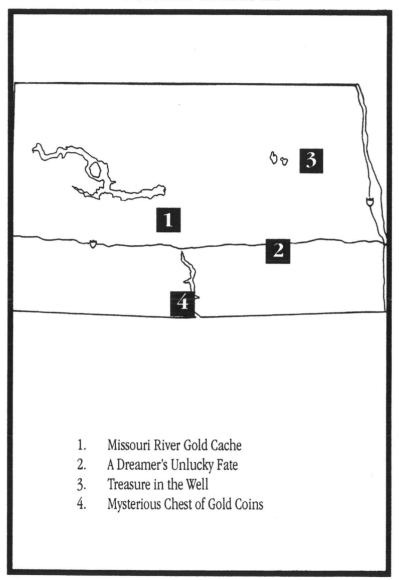

1. Missouri River Gold Cache
2. A Dreamer's Unlucky Fate
3. Treasure in the Well
4. Mysterious Chest of Gold Coins

Missouri River Gold Cache

During the late 1700s and early 1800s, hardy men, in search of wealth and adventure, left the relative comforts of the more populated and settled regions of the east and midwest and journeyed into rugged and remote portions of the Rocky Mountains. Braving harsh weather and Indians who resented their intrusion, they trapped beaver and other fur-bearing mammals, returning to civilization once each year to sell the pelts.

When they grew too old to trap any longer, many of these mountain men retired to St. Louis or some eastern city, content to live off the fortunes made from the beaver and regale avid listeners with adventurous and exciting tales of their lives among the Indians and wild animals.

Some chose to remain in the mountains, and they continued to trap the rivers and streams until they met death or the market for beaver disappeared. Some of these men returned penniless, but a few persistent others remained to seek their fortune in other ways—prospecting the granite outcrops of the range for precious metals. Searching for gold and silver was often just as risky as trapping beaver, and considerably more chancy, but now and then some made a fabulous strike.

It was one such party of fourteen Frenchmen, trappers who failed to find beaver in sufficient quantity, that discovered gold in a remote canyon stream bed in the Montana Rockies. For several months, the men panned nuggets from the sands and gravel at the bottom of the narrow stream, and, after several months of harvesting the rich stones, they filled several leather pouches with their take. Believing they now possessed wealth far beyond anything they had ever imagined, the Frenchmen decided to travel to St. Louis. Reaching the Missouri River, they purchased a plank boat and floated downstream for several days before reaching Fort Berthold in the fall of 1864. The fort, a well-known trading post, was located in western North Dakota in the heart of Sioux Indian country.

While resting up at Fort Berthold, the Frenchmen replenished their supplies and ammunition, paying for the goods with some of their gold nuggets. On the day scheduled for departure, many residents of the fort watched as the men loaded their equipment into the boat. The leather sacks filled with gold nuggets and placed in a wooden box that was closed and lashed down tightly near the rear of the vessel interested the onlookers. Prior to departing, the travelers were warned about warring Indians along the way. Numerous bands of Dakota Sioux camped near the river and were known to attack and kill whites who entered the region.

Late one afternoon several days later, the slow-moving craft sailed to a wooded area near the shore that looked as if it might offer a promising campsite. Nearby, the Knife River entered the Missouri from the west, mixing its silt-laden waters with those of the wider stream.

Unknown to the Frenchmen, a large contingent of Sioux was camped on the plain just beyond the dense woods. Two Sioux bowmen, hunting deer near a willow thicket along the riverbank, spotted the oncoming vessel and rushed back to the camp to alert the others. Within minutes, dozens of warriors, armed with bows and arrows, lances, and rifles, concealed themselves in the willows along the bank, poised for the arrival of the newcomers.

The moment the boat's prow struck the sandy bank, a trapper leaped out with a rope and secured it to a nearby willow tree. As the remaining occupants of the crowded vessel debarked, a volley of arrows and bullets fired from the willows instantly killed half of the Frenchmen. Two trappers ran frantically along the riverbank in an attempt to escape the onrushing Indians, but they were quickly overtaken and killed. Two others tried vainly to untie the boat and push out into the river, but they were slain before they could escape. Three of the men who survived the initial volley jumped into the Missouri River and swam to the other side, concealing themselves among a clutter of driftwood that had beached on the far shore.

In stunned silence, the survivors watched as several of the Indians lifted scalps from their fallen countrymen while others stripped them of their clothes and boots. Two warriors entered the boat and muttered exclamations of delight at finding the packs of foodstuffs. After discovering and examining the sacks of gold nuggets packed tightly into the wooden box, the Indians merely dropped them back into the container and abandoned the boat.

After throwing the victims' bodies into the river, the Indians gathered the scalps and booty and returned to their camp. As the sun settled low on the western horizon, the three Frenchmen, concealed among the logs and branches on the opposite shore, watched silently as the small wooden boat, still moored to the willow and containing nearly a quarter of a million dollars in gold, bobbed lazily in the current.

The next morning, the three survivors crept cautiously from their hiding place and fled on foot across the open plain toward the south. Their journey was fraught with terror and hardship. They suffered thirst and starvation, scorching days in the intense sun, and severely blistered feet. Occasionally, they encountered war parties and were forced to seek concealment in shallow ravines for hours at a time until the Indians passed. Along the way, two men perished, and the lone survivor was eventually discovered and nursed back to health by men on a passing wagon train.

When he was fit to travel again, the Frenchman enlisted the help of a friend and his son, and the three began to formulate plans to return to the confluence of the Knife and Missouri Rivers where they intended to retrieve the gold that was left in the boat.

Weeks later, as the three men neared the point where the attack had taken place, they were excited to discover the boat still floating in the shallows of the Missouri River, still secured to the same tree. Ecstatic, they abandoned caution and ran to the boat, opened the wooden box, and were rewarded by seeing the gold-filled pouches. Suddenly and without warning, a party of screaming Sioux charged from behind the willows and attacked the three intruders, firing repeatedly. The Frenchman was struck and killed instantly, his body toppling out of the boat and into the river. The other two dropped to the bottom of the boat and fired their revolvers over the gunwales at the charging Indians. Several Indian bullets pierced the wooden planking, one of them striking the father in the shoulder. Three Indians had been hit, and the warriors, dragging away their wounded, sought cover in the nearby trees.

As the boy applied a crude bandage to his father's wound, he noticed that the boat was sinking, water entering several holes created by stray bullets. Fearful they would either be shot by the Sioux or drown in the river, the two men slid out of the boat and quietly made their away along the bank, finally eluding the Indians. Several days later, the father died from his wound, and by the time the son reached civilization, he was half-crazed from his ordeal and never manifested any desire to return to the confluence of the Knife and Missouri Rivers to attempt to retrieve the gold.

Weeks passed, and news of the two Sioux attacks finally reached Fort Berthold. One of the traders who resided at the fort was keenly aware of the large fortune in gold carried by the Frenchmen and decided to travel to the area and see if he could recover it. Days later, he arrived at the Sioux village and parleyed with the chief, an old warrior named Fire Heart, for several hours. He knew many of the Indians from this band as they occasionally came to the fort to trade. After presenting the chief with a gift of tobacco, the trader requested permission to camp near the river and hunt. Suspecting nothing, the chief granted approval.

The next day, when he was certain no Indians were about, the trader searched along the riverbank hoping to find the Frenchmen's boat. Luck was with him, for he soon discovered the craft, still tied to the willow and half sunk in the shallow water, only the prow sticking out.

Stripping off his clothes, the trader waded out to the boat and, chest deep in water and feeling around with his toes, located the wooden box that he believed contained the gold. Taking a deep breath, he ducked below the surface, opened the box, and removed one of the gold-filled leather pouches. After carrying it to shore, he returned to the sunken craft several times until he had removed all of the gold.

Carrying the sacks to the foot of a large cottonwood tree, he scooped out a hole and buried all but one, which he placed in his saddlebags.

Days later when the trader returned to Fort Berthold, he became conspicuous almost immediately as a result of his new-found wealth. Drinking heavily, gambling, and spending lavishly one night, he informed anyone close enough to hear that he had located the gold of the massacred Frenchmen and intended to return to the secret cache for the rest of it. During the evening, however, the trader became involved in a fight during a card game and was stabbed to death.

Many believed that the only person who knew the location of the Frenchmen's gold was now dead, and the matter was quickly forgotten.

Weeks passed, and one day Chief Fire Heart, leader of the Sioux who had attacked and killed the Frenchmen, arrived at a remote trading post in central North Dakota to purchase some supplies. The Indian offered to pay with gold nuggets and poured out a large handful of them from a leather pouch he withdrew from beneath his blanket.

H.H. Larned, a customer at the trading post, saw the nuggets and asked Fire Heart where he had obtained them. The Indian told Larned he had found them, along with several others, buried next to a large tree near their former campsite on the Missouri River near the point where it is joined by the Knife River. At least twelve more pouches filled with gold still remained in the hole, the chief stated. Larned, along with several other men, planned to follow the Indians back to their camp in the hope of recovering some of the gold, but instead the tribe traveled northward into Canada.

In 1887, Fire Heart and his band returned to North Dakota and stopped at Fort Berthold to trade some buffalo robes for supplies. During the few days he remained near the fort, the chief told of how, many years earlier, his warriors attacked and killed the Frenchmen in the boat. He also related how he accidentally discovered the gold buried near the cottonwood tree.

When several of the listeners asked Fire Heart if any of the gold remained buried at the site, he told them yes and that he had removed only one of the pouches.

Fire Heart, an old man, died several weeks later. He never returned to the point near the Missouri River where he found the buried gold nuggets, an incredibly wealthy cache that remains hidden to this day.

A Dreamer's Unlucky Fate

Hermann Meir arrived in America from Germany in April 1867. He brought with him a dream of establishing a colony of thinkers and philosophers dedicated to leading kindred spirits to new intellectual heights, reorganizing existing political systems, and establishing a nation of greater peace and harmony. Meir also brought $40,000 worth of gold coins in a trunk with the rest of his few belongings.

Hermann Meir was born, raised, and educated in Hannover, Germany, the seventh of seven children and the only boy. Hermann's father, Wolfgang Meir, was a successful businessman, banker, and local political leader, who amassed a large fortune as a result of shrewd trade practices and business decisions. The elder Meir also made sure all of his children were educated at the region's finest institutions. Hermann was a particular source of pride to the wealthy German.

While attending the academy, young Hermann, only thirteen years old, became fascinated with the discipline of philosophy. By the time he was fifteen, he was extremely well-read on the subject and capable of extended and sophisticated debates with his instructors. More often than not, the young Meir won the discussions.

As the years passed, the youthful, energetic Meir grew and matured to become an idealistic dreamer of a perfect world. As he looked around and examined his country in the light of his learning, he perceived that Germany, indeed, all of Europe, was falling into ruin and that the people were doomed to unhappiness, political corruption, and fascism. As Meir preached about establishing a utopia—a perfect world for intellectuals—he gathered an impressive following. Soon, hundreds attended Meir's lectures. They went to hear his message and, along with their charismatic lecturer, dreamed of a better world.

Meir decided that his utopia would have to be established outside of Europe and began to consider the possibilities of taking his movement to America. After days of discussions with his converts, he arranged to borrow $40,000 in gold from his father to finance his search for and construction of a colony in some isolated part of the rapidly growing and developing United States, where he could perpetuate and refine his philosophies and teachings and send his followers forth to convert others.

Bidding his growing legion farewell, Meir departed for America, promising to send for the faithful followers as soon as he located a suitable site for his colony.

After a long and uneventful Atlantic crossing, Meir disembarked in New York City and spent several weeks in the area becoming comfortable with the new language and studying the habits and philosophies of the citizens. Disgusted at what he considered the filth and corruption he encountered in the large city, as well as the poorly developed intellect, Meir decided his colony, if it was to be successful, needed to be located far from the negative influences that reigned here, far from the sin and temptation of places like New York City.

Asking discrete questions to traders, trappers, hunters, and explorers who had traveled in the far west and Great Plains, Meir learned about the existence of vast expanses of land—rolling plains and fertile prairies—particularly in the region of the Dakotas. He listened to the tales of rich soil, extending from horizon to horizon, suitable for large grain farms and grazing lands necessary for the support of his colony. According to the travelers, all of this land was there for the taking. The only obstacles, they warned, were the Indian tribes who resisted the encroachment of whites into their territory.

Meir naively believed he would be able to convert the Indians to his way of thinking. He felt certain these children of the wilderness would see the logic of his arguments and the hope for the future in his philosophies. He intended to convert the Indians to his beliefs and offer them jobs in his new colony. Hermann Meir had his plans well-formulated in his own mind. But Meir, as brilliant as he was, was completely ignorant in the ways of the plains Indians. He knew absolutely nothing about the Sioux who roamed and hunted the Great Plains. If he had, he would have reconsidered his plan.

After residing in New York City for about four months, Meir purchased a heavy wagon and a team of horses, loaded his belongings into it, and struck out for the region he had selected for his new colony—the northern plains of North Dakota. Meir was firm in his idea of his destiny, but his exact destination was still obscure.

For weeks, Meir endured hardships as he traveled toward the Dakotas. Rainstorms occasionally washed out the roads, flood waters often swelled streams and prevented his crossing for days at a time, wild animals terrorized his horses, and bandits rode the trails in search of easy prey. Indians were occasionally sighted, but none ever approached the solo traveler.

Meir eventually arrived at a tiny Scandinavian settlement in central Minnesota where he rested for several weeks before continuing. Despite repeated warnings about what the Swedes referred to as the "savage heathens" who lived on the Great Plains to the west, Meir was unconcerned. His hopes and dreams, he told them, were all wrapped up in his establishment of a new utopia, and nothing could deter him. Thanking his new friends for their hospitality, Meir reloaded the wagon, lashed his trunk full of gold coins down to the wagon bed, and traveled into the Dakotas.

As he rode high upon the hard wooden wagon seat, Meir regarded the vast rolling plains that stretched out in all directions and dreamed of the new city he would build. At first, he would construct a humble sod house. When the time was right, he would plant the seeds he had brought and establish the beginnings of what would eventually evolve into vast fields of grain. With the fortune in gold coins he carried, he planned to purchase and arrange for the delivery of materials, which would be used to begin construction on his city, and cattle that would graze on the lush prairie grasses. After a firm and solid beginning was established, Meir would then send for his followers in Germany who patiently awaited word from their leader.

One afternoon, Meir guided his horses along the periphery of a large buffalo herd in an area located approximately twenty miles southwest of the present-day town of Carrington, North Dakota. Cresting a low rise, he halted his wagon and gazed upon a scene that froze the blood in his veins. A band of thirty brightly painted and feathered Indians rode toward him. On spotting Meir, the leader of the party raised a long, iron-tipped lance and uttered a piercing scream. Instantly, the entire horde kicked their mounts toward the German, brandishing bows, rifles, and lances.

The intent of the Indians was perfectly clear to Meir and for a moment he forgot all of his brilliant philosophies and hopes. All he could think about was fleeing from these wrathful attackers. Turning his wagon, Meir whipped his weary team in a futile attempt to escape. In a matter of mere minutes, however, they were upon him. Three Indians leaped into the wagon while several others grabbed the traces of the horses and pulled them to a halt in the middle of a large buffalo wallow.

Meir stood up in the front of the wagon and held his arms outward in a gesture of submission. His response came from a tall, muscular Indian wearing nothing but a breechclout, moccasins, and a cluster of three feathers in his braided hair. As Meir began to speak, the Indian thrust a lance into his chest with such force that nearly two feet of it protruded from the German's back. His eyes widened in surprise and shock, and Meir tried to speak but only blood gurgled from his quivering mouth. A second later he toppled from the wagon, dead before he struck the ground.

The Indians quickly detached the horses from their traces and began to rifle the belongings in the wagon. While some of them distributed the few items of clothing, others fought over Meir's boots, hat, and jacket.

The same Indian who had killed Meir discovered the pile of bright shiny gold coins in the bottom of the trunk and lifted out a handful of them to examine. Finding no apparent utility in the objects, he contemptuously tossed them into the buffalo wallow.

Within minutes, anything perceived of having any value to the Indians was either being worn or tied to some of the ponies. Before riding away, two Indians set fire to the wagon. As the war party returned toward the direction where they had first been seen by Meir, none looked back to watch the flaming wagon and the billowing smoke rising into the cooling afternoon air.

For several hours past sundown, the glow of the smoldering wagon could be seen for several miles on the prairie. Little was left save for the iron fittings, wheel rims, and the unburned portions of a few planks. All that was left of Meir's trunk was the metal corners, hinges, and the hand-made hasp. Most of the gold coins had fused into a solid mass from the heat of the fire and settled to the bottom of a pile of ashes.

Years later when travelers and settlers passed the buffalo wallow, they would recall the story often heard in the east of the idealistic German philosopher who traveled alone to the wild Dakotas to establish a city. It was only many years later that people learned about the gold that Hermann Meir carried with him. By the time fortune hunters arrived in the central North Dakota region, no one could remember the exact buffalo wallow in which Meir met his death.

Gold worth $40,000 in 1867 would carry a value many times that today, and it is likely that some North Dakota wheat farmer has come close enough to the fortune to touch it with the tip of his plow.

Hermann Meir's dreams of a colony are gone and mostly forgotten, but his fortune remains close to the site he would likely have selected for his followers. The gold still lies just beneath the soil in some long-forgotten buffalo wallow in the North Dakota plains waiting for a lucky and patient searcher.

Treasure in the Well

Gustav Halverson, a merry semi-recluse, lived for many years alone in a big farmhouse on the North Dakota plains in Nelson County. Halverson, allegedly a wealthy man, arrived from his native Sweden years earlier and settled on the Dakota prairie where he owned and operated a large wheat farm. Halverson employed several workers, but they rarely saw the old Swede who preferred to remain in his big house seated in his vast library reading his favorite books. Halverson was rarely seen in Grand Forks, the nearest large city. On the few times he visited town each year, it was to order books.

On the rare occasions Halverson was seen outdoors, he was usually standing by his well. When he settled into this relatively isolated location, one of his first tasks was to dig a well for fresh water. Completely by himself, Halverson excavated the well nearly sixty feet deep. When he struck water, he hauled rocks in from miles away to line the excavation and keep it from collapsing inward.

As more and more people settled on the Dakota prairie, the Grand Forks to Minot Road—a trail that cut across a portion of the northeastern part of the state—was the principal artery for travelers. On many occasions, westward migrants stopped at the Halverson farm to rest and water themselves and their livestock. Halverson always greeted such visitors with great enthusiasm, personally led them to his well, and showed them how to draw the cool, clear water. He always appeared excited about having visitors and saw to their every need. But when they departed, he returned to the house remaining there for days.

When automobiles began to replace the horse- and ox-drawn wagons, Halverson's farmhouse still attracted visitors who needed water for their overheated radiators. As in former days, the old Swede greeted his visitors with a smile and happily shared his water with them, always showing off his well with great pride.

One summer, Halverson had not been seen for a period of several weeks, and one of his employees entered the big farmhouse looking for him. When he did, he discovered that the old man had been dead for several days.

For weeks following Halverson's death, authorities conducted an extensive search in this country and Europe for heirs to his land and fortune but were unable to locate any. Apparently, the Swede had no known living relatives.

Though it was well-known in this part of North Dakota that Halverson was extremely wealthy, none of the banks in the state held an account for him. On further investigation, authorities finally located a banker in Grand Forks who told them that, years earlier, Halverson had come into his bank early one morning and had his entire savings converted into gold coins. It took several weeks for the transaction to be completed, but when the Swede rode out of town he carried with him, according to the banker, more than a million dollars in gold.

Under strict supervision, Halverson's farmhouse, barn, and grounds were searched, but his fortune was not found. Whatever became of the old Swede's money remained a mystery for many years.

Eventually, the Halverson farm went into receivership and new owners took it over. Because the old house showed signs of advanced decay, it was torn down and the new owners con- structed a residence about a mile away. The old well that Halverson had been so proud of was filled in. Years passed, and the prairie grasses reclaimed the Swede's homesite.

Several years following Gustav Halverson's death, a man attending an auction in Bemidji, Minnesota, purchased an old wooden trunk for about five dollars. It was a rather common-looking trunk—nothing distinctive about it at all—but the buyer believed it would be useful for storing tools. After paying for it, the man loaded the trunk into his vehicle and drove home. After unloading it, he opened the trunk and was surprised to find it filled with old photographs, legal papers, and a thick journal.

The buyer did not recognize anyone in the photographs, which were typical of the kind taken by professional photographers during the late 1800s and early 1900s. The legal papers were all in a foreign language he believed was German. The journal, however, was written in English in a handsome script, and it detailed the life and interests of one Gustav Halverson.

Reading the journal, the trunk's buyer realized he held in his hands the autobiography of a man who apparently owned a large wheat farm in Nelson County, North Dakota, read many good books, and was very wealthy. At one point in the journal, the reader grew very interested when he read how well over a million dollars' worth of currency had been converted into gold and hidden in a rock-lined well located somewhere on the farm. Excited at the possibility of locating and retrieving the gold, the reader studied the journal further in an attempt to determine the location of the old farm and the well.

No date could be found anywhere in the journal, so the reader had no idea how old it was. The journal, however, contained a description of the approximate location of the farmhouse. Several days later, the reader traveled to Nelson County with hopes of recovering the gold.

Arriving at the location he thought Halverson's farmhouse once stood, the reader found nothing except low, rolling hills covered with prairie grasses. After two days of making inquiries, he finally located the current owners of the land who had a vague idea of the old Halverson homesite.

Though the owner of the journal searched throughout the region for several days, he was unable to find the old well that contained the incredible fortune in gold coins.

Mysterious Chest of Gold Coins

Arnie Jorgensen knew he wasn't cut out for farming when, as a young lad, he followed his father and brothers around the grain fields in their European homeland. After arriving in America and settling on the vast Minnesota prairie, the Jorgensen clan continued to pursue what they knew—planting and harvesting cereal crops—but young Arnie spent his time daydreaming or hiding from his father, unwilling to spend his days toiling in the beating sun, driving wind, and icy cold of the northern plains.

When he was twenty years old, Arnie Jorgensen bade his family goodbye, informing them he was going to travel west to the Black Hills of South Dakota where he intended to mine gold and become wealthy. His parents could barely hold back tears when the young man climbed atop his stout horse and took the lead rein of the pack mule. His mother handed him a woolen vest she had knitted, kissed his hand, and stepped back. As the fair-haired Swede rode away, his father and mother held hands and watched him from the front porch of their home, praying for God to watch over their son. It was the last time they ever saw him.

Jorgensen's journey across western Minnesota and into the North Dakota plains was, for the most part, uneventful. During the long days as he rode along, he dreamed of the wealth he believed awaited him in the Black Hills. He would use this wealth to find a new life of excitement, ease, luxury, and comfort, a life where one did not have to toil from sunrise until past sunset in the wheat fields. Arnie Jorgensen wanted to be rich, and he wanted all that went along with it—fine homes, groomed horses, tailored suits, and high society.

Several days after leaving the Minnesota farm, Jorgensen arrived at the tiny settlement of Valley City, North Dakota, where he purchased a few supplies. He visited with citizens and shopkeepers, excitedly telling them of his plans to pan gold from the streams of the Black Hills. The morning he left Valley City was bright with only a slight breeze, but for some reason the young man grew uncomfortable with a rapidly growing premonition of disaster. That evening as he cooked his supper over a low campfire far out on the prairie, he became very nervous and was certain someone was watching him. He did not sleep at all that night or the next—or for many nights thereafter. He confessed his feelings of discomfort to the few travelers he encountered along the way.

Late one evening days later, Jorgensen arrived at the banks of the Missouri River near a point where it flowed into South Dakota. Not wishing to cross the wide stream in the dark, he chose to make camp nearby. After staking his animals and eating his dinner, Jorgensen rolled into his blanket and tried to sleep but only spent another fitful night, unable to shake the feeling something bad was about to happen to him.

When morning arrived, Jorgensen ate hard bread and drank coffee for breakfast. Enjoying the pleasant weather, he decided to take a walk up a nearby ravine, following the tracks made by various animals the previous night.

Rounding a bend in the narrow, steep-sided ravine, Jorgensen spotted some graying, rotted wooden planks sticking out of the soft bottom. Walking over to the site, the young man recognized the remains of a wagon, one that apparently fell into the ravine years earlier. When he pulled one of the wagon planks from the loose sands of the ravine bottom, he noticed an arrowhead embedded in one side. Several more planks yielded other arrowheads and Jorgensen concluded that the wagon had been attacked by Indians many years earlier. As the young Swede dug in the rotted debris, he uncovered several bones, all of them human.

As it was now mid-morning, Jorgensen realized he must soon gather up the horse and mule and be on his way. Just as he prepared to leave, he noticed the corner of a rectangular object partially buried in the dirt next to the rotted boards. Scraping away some of the covering sand, he was surprised to find a small wooden chest. Lifting it from the ground, he found it much heavier than expected, and he could hear the clank and jingle of metal coming from within. As he appraised the chest, he observed it was well-made with finely-tooled metal fittings. The hasp that held it closed was not fitted with a lock, so Jorgensen pried it up and lifted the lid. There, hundreds of gold coins—an impressive fortune—filled the entire chest.

As Jorgensen stared at the gold coins, he imagined they represented the total wealth of the unfortunate family traveling westward in the wagon that now lay rotted and in pieces in this ravine. Attacked by Indians, the entire family was undoubtedly killed or taken captive, and the wagon, after the horses were cut loose, was rolled over the steep bank and into the gorge. The Indians likely ransacked the wagon, but they ignored the heavy chest.

Jorgensen's reverie was broken by the sudden presence of a shadow on the ravine's wall. Rising quickly and turning around, his heart leaped as he gazed into the hostile eyes of twenty Sioux Indians on horseback in a line along the rim of the opposite wall. Terrified and completely unarmed, Jorgensen stood wide-eyed and unmoving. Before he could collect his thoughts, however, his body was immediately pierced by at least a dozen arrows. After finally discovering wealth such as he had always dreamed of, Arnie Jorgensen collapsed to his knees next to the fortune in the rotted chest. Momentarily he gazed at the shining wealth before him as blood gushed out of his mouth and splattered onto several of the coins. Then, with a final shudder, the young Swede fell dead.

Seconds later, an Indian ripped the blonde scalp from Jorgensen's head as several others fought over his boots, pants, and woolen vest.

An elderly Dakota Sioux who claimed to have been a member of the war party that killed Arnie Jorgensen told the young man's story in 1919. The Indian also admitted that he had been part of a larger war party, which attacked the wagon that Jorgensen had found lying at the bottom of the ravine. According to the old warrior, the chest filled with gold coins was still lying in the ravine near the Missouri River close to the South Dakota border as late as 1917.

The original owners of the chest filled with what must have been an incredible fortune has remained a mystery and yet unsolved by researchers. From all available evidence, the gold still lies at the bottom of the steep-sided ravine that is apparently an ephemeral tributary to the Missouri River somewhere in south-central North Dakota.

Oklahoma

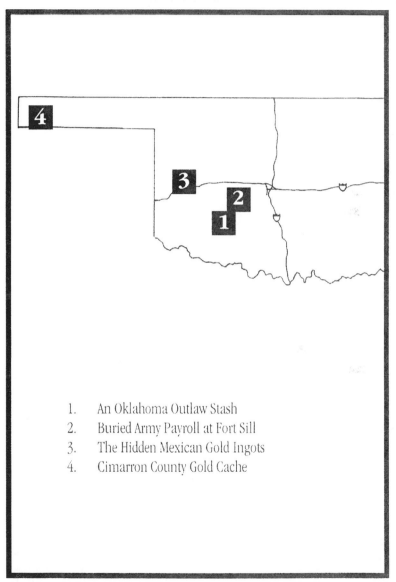

1. An Oklahoma Outlaw Stash
2. Buried Army Payroll at Fort Sill
3. The Hidden Mexican Gold Ingots
4. Cimarron County Gold Cache

An Oklahoma Outlaw Stash

The man who lay dying on the hospital cot was only dimly aware that other people bustled about in the room. He heard voices, but they sounded as if they were passing through water. He was vaguely aware that it was daylight, but his vision and perceptions were clouded by pain and morphine. Once, when he regained consciousness for a few moments, he thought he sensed the image of a nurse bent over him, wiping his hot face with a cool rag and murmuring soft, soothing words in a singsong cadence. The man tried to speak, but his parched throat and cracked and broken lips fought the words, keeping them trapped within. Finally, with great difficulty he managed to weakly rasp the words "the money," "buried," "friends dead"—cryptic utterances that only mildly aroused the nurse's curiosity at the time.

The patient, about thirty-five years old, wandered in and out of consciousness for the next two weeks, his only companion was the nurse he saw the first time he opened his eyes. Weakly, he sometimes attempted to reach out to her. Other times he tried to talk, but after the first few words, he lapsed once more into unconsciousness.

Though the patient seldom remained lucid for more than a few minutes at a time, he was aware he was dying. From several places on his body he felt the pain and the itch of the numerous wounds he had received days earlier. By the time the surgeon had examined, cleaned, and bandaged the wounds, he had removed a total of seven bullets and three arrowheads. Many of the projectiles had reached vital organs and the loss of blood had been critical. As the unconscious man was carried from the operating table to a cot in a corner room of the tiny hospital, the doctor told the attending nurses he didn't believe the man would live through the night.

Miraculously, the patient, who possessed no identification, clung tenaciously to life for several more days. From time to time, he would thrash about on the cot, screaming, his eyes wide with fear. Once, when the nurse visited him to change his bandages, she thought she saw tears in his eyes.

One day as the nurse spoon-fed the dying man some broth, he rose clumsily to a seated position and looked around confused. As the nurse helped him lay back down and placed a pillow comfortably behind his head, he reached out and gently took her hand, begging her to sit with him awhile.

For nearly an hour, the woman remained, not a word spoken between them. Finally, the stranger looked up at the woman seated beside him and asked permission to explain how he came to be in the hospital and how he acquired the wounds. As she listened patiently, the dying man unfolded an incredible story of a bank robbery, a frightening escape across the Oklahoma prairie, a deadly fight with Indians, the death of his two companions, and the hasty burial of a fortune in gold and silver coins.

About two months earlier, the dying man, who referred to himself only as John, was returning from the buffalo range with two companions he called Kelley and Morton. Having made their living as hide hunters for years, the three long-time friends had gradually grown disappointed at the dwindling herds of the great shaggy animals and decided it was time to find some other kind of work. The problem was that none of the three had ever done much of anything except hunting and skinning buffalo.

One evening while seated around a campfire somewhere on the broad yellow prairie in western Kansas, one of the men suggested they rob a bank. After discussing their bad luck and discovering they had less than five dollars between them and no chance of finding work, the notion of robbing a bank took on significance.

Arriving in the bustling city of Wichita several days later, the three men set up camp just outside town and for the next three days rode into Wichita to observe the comings and goings of bank employees and customers. Finally, they decided to rob the bank when it opened the following morning.

At precisely nine o'clock, the owner of the bank was unlocking the front door when John walked up and shoved the barrel of his pistol into his back and hastened him inside. Kelley followed while Morton stood guard outside. Within a matter of minutes, several canvas bags were filled with gold and silver coins from the bank's safe, and the owner was tied, gagged, and shoved to the floor behind his desk. Carrying the heavy sacks, the three bandits ran to their horses, mounted, and fled from the town.

For the next two days, they traveled in a southerly direction, riding hard and stopping only to let their animals water and graze. John, Kelley, and Morton subsisted on old biscuits made in camp days earlier. Their horses, unaccustomed to the added weight of the heavy sacks of coins, occasionally faltered and stumbled.

The three outlaws crossed the Kansas state line and entered Indian Territory on the afternoon of the third day of hard riding, and when they were certain they were not being followed, they stopped in a grove of elms beside the trail and set up camp.

Around the campfire that night, the three friends counted the money they had taken from the bank and were surprised and delighted to discover they escaped with nearly $50,000 in gold and silver coins. They decided to travel together to Texas and use the money to set themselves up with a fine ranch.

For the next several days, the outlaws continued on an erratic southerly course heading toward Texas. One afternoon while riding across the open prairie, Morton's horse grew lame and slower. The men feared that if the animal could not continue, Morton would be forced to walk and his share of the loot would have to be divided and carried by the other two horses.

As the travelers passed through a region near present-day Caddo County, Kelley recalled a time several years earlier when he had traveled through the nearby Wichita Mountains. There, he told his friends, they would be able to find fresh water, shelter, and wild game while men and horses alike rested from the tiresome journey.

Their stay in the Wichita Mountains, however, was not as peaceful as they hoped. From the day the three men arrived, they could see Indians silently watching them from nearby ridges. Kelley recognized them as Comanches and told his companions they were regarded as the most bloodthirsty Indians ever to reside on the Great Plains. Camp that night was subdued and quiet, and none of the men got much sleep.

After the third day of resting in the Wichita Mountains, the three outlaws packed up and continued their journey. Though the lame horse still struggled with the heavy load, it was able to walk at a cautious pace.

Late that afternoon the men stopped at a spring. As the horses watered and the men ate biscuits, Morton spotted about forty mounted warriors two miles back on the trail they had just traveled and advancing rapidly. Quickly, the outlaws climbed into their saddles and spurred their mounts southward. As soon as the Comanches spotted the fleeing riders, they charged toward them, yelling and brandishing lances, rifles, and bows and arrows.

After riding only a few hundred yards, it became obvious to the outlaws that their heavily-laden mounts could never outdistance the swift plains-bred ponies of the Comanches. Morton suggested they cut the sacks of money loose to lighten the load, but the other two resisted the idea.

Suddenly, Morton's crippled horse could continue no farther and collapsed on the grassy turf, throwing rider and money to the ground. John and Kelley turned their horses, dismounted, and, along with Morton, took shelter behind the fallen animal. As the lame horse kicked furiously and tried to rise, Kelley shot it through the head. Seconds later, the Comanches reined up about a hundred yards away and began firing bullets and arrows at the three men hunkered behind the dead animal. For nearly an hour the outlaws kept their heads down, cowering behind their accidental and insufficient shelter. Morton, believing a show of courage and firepower might frighten away the Indians, rose up and took aim at a cluster of Comanches. Almost immediately, he was struck in the abdomen by a bullet fired from the left. Bleeding profusely, he dropped to the ground, moaning in pain.

For the next several hours, the Indians lofted arrows in a high, wide parabola toward their enemy and fired away at the dead horse with rifles. Blood from the animal splattered onto the defenders, and the horse soon resembled a pincushion with at least a hundred arrows piercing its hide.

The warriors with guns took up positions around the defensive position in an attempt to get a clean shot at the white men, but fortunately, the outlaws had sufficient ammunition and aim to force the Indians to maintain a respectable distance.

Around sunset, Morton died from his wound. As John and Kelley lay in terrified silence next to their dead companion, the Comanches retreated about a mile and a half north up the trail, where they set up a camp for the night.

When it grew dark, John and Kelley saw campfires in the distance and presumed the Comanches had abandoned the fight until morning. Using their belt knives and their hands, the two scooped out a shallow hole and buried Morton.

For several more hours the two men sat in the dark considering their options when Kelley suggested they make a run for it. While John kept watch on the Indian camp in the distance, Kelley went in search of the horses. Within minutes, he found them grazing a short distance away, still saddled and burdened with bank robbery loot. When Kelley returned with the mounts, the two men retrieved Mortons share of the heist and distributed it between the two remaining steeds. Once the horses were loaded, the two men mounted and slipped away toward the south.

Just as they abandoned the barely significant protection afforded by Morton's dead horse, a hint of dawn appeared on the eastern horizon, barely illuminating the stark prairie. The two men had covered a little more than a mile when they heard the screams of the Indians in pursuit. Lashing and spurring their horses, each one now encumbered with even more weight than before, the outlaws tried to coax the animals to greater speeds.

But it was not to happen, for within minutes the Indians were almost upon them. Kelley spotted an old buffalo wallow beside the trail and led John toward it. With hardly any protection at all, they dismounted and took up positions flat on their bellies just below the rim of the depression and fired into the attacking line of Comanches, killing several. In the process, both John and Kelley received several wounds from Comanche bullets and arrows.

For the rest of the day, the Indians launched several frontal attacks only to be repelled by the bullets of their quarry. Around noon, Kelley was killed when a bullet slammed into his face. Though he had lost a great deal of blood from several wounds,

John was able to maintain his defensive position until sundown, at which time the Indians once again retreated some distance away to set up camp.

For the second night in a row, John buried a friend. Into a shallow hole he painfully excavated, he placed his long-time trail companion along with his saddle, two pistols, and rifle.

After covering the crude grave with dirt, John noticed the two horses grazing nearby. He retrieved them and led them to a nearby rise in the prairie where a lone tree grew. Here, he untied the sacks of coins and, though considerably weakened from loss of blood, dug a second hole into which he placed the entire robbery loot. Following this, he turned one of the horses loose, climbed aboard the other, and continued on toward Texas. Within only a few minutes after riding away from the only tree that could be seen on the prairie, he crossed what he identified as West Cache Creek, a landmark he intended to use when he returned to dig up the fortune in coins buried on the low rise in the prairie.

Somehow, John was able to ford the Red River and finally, several days later, arrived in Dallas. He was found lying in the middle of the town's main street early one morning with blood from his constantly reopened wounds seeping into the dirt. His horse was nowhere to be found.

When John finished relating his tale to the nurse, he sighed and told her he realized he would never be able to return for the money. He asked her to find it and return it to the bank in Wichita. Before falling asleep, he thanked the nurse for her kindness. Two days later, John died in his sleep.

Several years later, the nurse resigned her position at the hospital, organized a small expedition party, and set forth into Indian Territory in an attempt to find the fortune in coins buried by the dead outlaw. Following directions she gleaned from John's description of the region, she concentrated her search in an area approximately four miles west-southwest of the present-day town of Geronimo near the line that separates Comanche and Cotton Counties. The landscape she encountered in this region closely matched the descriptions provided by John, but her party was constantly harassed by local Indians and she abandoned the search.

A few more years passed and the Territory was eventually opened up for settlement. Believing it was now safe to travel into this part of Oklahoma, the nurse organized a second expedition to try and locate the treasure. This time, she found what she believed was the actual site where the three bank robbers defended themselves against the Comanches while taking shelter behind the dead horse, but from that point she was unable to interpret the rest of John's directions. Frustrated at every turn, she finally decided to abandon the search and return to Dallas.

For years, only a handful of people were aware of the story of the outlaw's flight from the Comanches and the subsequent caching of the robbery loot on the prairie. Those that did were intrigued by an article that appeared in the October 18, 1907, issue of the Lawton, Oklahoma, *Daily News-Republican*. Under the headline "Human Form Unearthed In Big Pasture," the article related how two Cotton County farmers found the muzzle of a rifle sticking out of the ground and decided to investigate. After digging just a few inches into the soil, they found, in addition to the rifle, a human skeleton, two pistols, and a saddle. The saddle was described as being in fairly good condition, and when it was cleaned, the name A.E. Kelley was seen branded onto the skirts.

To those who were aware of the significance of this find, it meant that the treasure was buried nearby on a low rise in the prairie on which grew a solitary tree. Unfortunately, the two farmers refused to reveal the location where they discovered the skeleton, saying only that it was near an old buffalo wallow not far from West Cache Creek.

In 1910, another startling discovery was made. Less than three miles north of the site where Kelley's remains were found, a second skeleton was discovered when runoff from a severe rainstorm eroded a shallow incision into the surface of the prairie. This skeleton was found at the exact location the nurse believed the three outlaws initially defended themselves against the attacking Comanches. The remains were undoubtedly Morton's.

To date, there is no evidence that the nearly $50,000 in gold and silver coins buried on the Oklahoma plains near West Cache Creek has ever been discovered. This huge cache apparently still lies unclaimed and is now worth several times its original value.

Buried Army Payroll at Fort Sill

It was early in the morning of a warm June day in 1892 when the payroll stagecoach rumbled along the well-traveled dirt road toward Fort Sill. The coach left Wichita Falls, Texas, just before sunrise, and as the driver guided the horses northeastward, his only thoughts were of a safe crossing of the Red River and arriving at the military post in the allotted three days. Accompanied by two shotgun-toting guards riding next to the driver, the stagecoach carried nearly $100,000 in gold and silver coins, which was intended as part of the month's payroll for the fort.

The driver and two guards had covered this same route on seven previous occasions, each involved with delivering a payroll and each uneventful. Initially, a mounted military escort consisting of six to twelve armed soldiers accompanied the payroll coach, but as the months passed and no threat to the cargo ever materialized, the large guard was withdrawn.

On this morning, however, as the relaxed driver and guards sat atop the spring seat of the coach joking and smoking, a trio of masked riders suddenly appeared from behind a cluster of trees, shot the two lead horses pulling the coach, and wounded one of the guards.

When one of the outlaws ordered the three men off the coach, the second guard grabbed his shotgun and fired at the mounted bandits, killing two of them instantly. The third outlaw, wounded badly in the shoulder and chest, shot and killed the guard.

After ordering the driver and the wounded guard to lie face-down on the ground, the remaining outlaw, bleeding badly, removed six heavy saddlebags of coins from beneath the driver's seat and loaded them onto his dead companions' horses. He then instructed the two men to begin walking back to Wichita Falls and, with the two payroll-laden horses in tow, continued along the trail to the northeast.

Though he originally intended to travel to Oklahoma City with the stolen payroll, the outlaw, suffering great pain and loss of blood, decided to seek medical help. The closest physician was located at Fort Sill, so daringly, he rode toward the military post.

The bandit arrived at the fort just after sundown on the following day and stopped at a well near the side of the trading post. As he watered his horses, he looked around for some suitable place to hide the money, because he knew if he were caught with the payroll he would be hung.

Making certain that no one was mingling about on this warm and moonless night, the outlaw strode a total of ten paces from the well, scooped out a hole just deep enough to contain the coin-filled saddlebags, and deposited them within. After filling the hole, he walked his horses back and forth across the surface to remove any indication of the recent excavation. After receiving treatment for his wound, he decided, he would return to the site, remove the payroll, and continue to Oklahoma City.

The outlaw identified himself to the post surgeon only as Allen and told him he had been injured in a hunting accident. After plucking buckshot from the wounds and covering them with bandages, the doctor gave Allen an injection for his pain and suggested he try to get some sleep on the cot in the office. Weak from loss of blood, the long horseback journey, no sleep, and the medication, Allen dropped into a deep slumber.

It didn't take long for the news about the robbery to reach Fort Sill. By the time Allen had arrived at the post, several high-ranking officers had been advised of the holdup, and at least six platoons were combing the countryside searching for some sign of the surviving bandit. The driver and the wounded guard were on their way to the fort even as Allen was being treated by the surgeon.

The next morning, the driver and guard identified Allen's horse as belonging to one of the outlaws who had robbed the coach. Allen was quickly arrested, tried, found guilty, and sentenced to prison at Huntsville, Texas, where he remained for the next thirty-three years.

When Allen was finally released from prison in 1925, the first thing he did was seek work. Eventually, he landed a job on a farm near Levelland, a small town in the Texas Panhandle, but at the first opportunity, he returned to Fort Sill and tried to recover the rich payroll he had buried near the well so many years before.

Though Fort Sill had changed dramatically during the more than three decades since Allen had last visited it, the ex-convict was able to locate the site of the old trading post and the well. Three factors, however, served to discourage Allen's quest for the treasure: it appeared that at least four to six feet of fill dirt had been added to the yard; the old outlaw could not remember which direction from the well he paced off ten steps; and a military guard considered him a vagrant and escorted him off the post. Discouraged, Allen returned to Levelland but continued to make plans to journey once again to Oklahoma and recover the treasure.

Several more years passed, and though Allen never gave up on his desire to recover the treasure cache, he never found the opportunity to return to Fort Sill. During that time, he became close friends with G. W. Cottrell, the owner of a neighboring farm. When Allen decided he could trust Cottrell, he told him about the robbery of the payroll stage and the subsequent burial of the loot. Allen gave Cottrell directions to the huge cache and told him that he should try to find it. Allen admitted to his friend that he was too old to do anything with the fortune even if he did recover it. A few months later Allen passed away.

As soon as his cotton crop was in, Cottrell, seventy-two years old, traveled to Fort Sill. After spending a few days looking around the military post, he entered the office of Master Sergeant Morris Swett, the post historian and librarian and explained his purpose. Swett introduced Cottrell to higher ranking officials who told the old farmer to fill out several pages of forms requesting permission to dig for treasure on military property. After doing so, Cottrell returned to Levelland to await approval, and several weeks later he was notified he would be allowed to carry out his search.

On January 27, 1937, Cottrell returned to Fort Sill and located the site of the old well—now filled in—in one corner of a maintenance building located near the intersection of McBride and Cureton Streets. The trading post had long since been torn down.

Having no idea of the direction and distance from the well the payroll had been buried, Cottrell could only guess at its location. Using only shovels, he supervised the excavation of several deep holes a few feet north of the well but found nothing.

Deciding he needed to employ some heavy equipment in order to increase his chances of recovering the buried coins, Cottrell returned to Levelland with the intention of contracting material and workers to aid him in his search.

Illness and the obligations of running his farm kept Cottrell in Levelland for the next several years, and in September 1940, he decided to share the secret of the buried treasure with his friend Van Webb. After writing a letter of introduction to Fort Sill officials, Cottrell financed Webb's trip to the military post to try and find the treasure. Webb, however, was not authorized to conduct an excavation and was sent away.

A month later, Cottrell, accompanied by Webb and a woman named Edna Crowder, returned to the military post. While Webb employed a divining rod to try and find the buried coins, Crowder consulted a crystal ball. The trio was unsuccessful and went back to Texas, never to return.

The matter of the buried payroll was dropped and quickly forgotten by most until April 1, 1964, when the army announced it had sufficient evidence of a buried payroll's existence and would try to recover it.

Employing bulldozers and augers, army engineers excavated a total of fifteen holes, each ten feet deep, in an area just south of the maintenance building. Nothing was found.

Those who observed the army's attempts at recovering the treasure were appalled at the unprofessional and careless manner in which the excavation was conducted. Many were dismayed that, after only digging into a relatively small area, the army completely abandoned the search.

Historians and treasure researchers are convinced of the truth of Allen's claim that the treasure was buried near the well and that it rests there today. Repeated requests over the past twenty-five years by interested individuals for permission to search for the treasure have been denied by Fort Sill officials who claim there is nothing to gain from a renewed excavation.

Nothing, says one researcher, except for a fortune in gold and silver coins.

The Hidden Mexican Gold Ingots

For more than two hundred and fifty years preceding the Civil War, dozens of major and minor routes crisscrossed the Great Plains along which traders, trappers, soldiers, Indians, and settlers traveled. Many of those who found gold and silver in the Rocky Mountains often utilized these roads to make the long journeys to St. Louis or New Orleans where they would sell the ore or ingots. It has been estimated by researchers that untold millions of dollars in precious metal was carried across the prairies to the growing cities in the east and south. Some travelers, however, were unsuccessful in transporting their fortunes across the prairie. As a result of depredations by bandits and Indians, some of it was lost, some of it was stolen, and some of it was hidden in caches along the way.

One story of an incredible fortune in gold ingots involves a Mexican pack train transporting well over three million dollars' worth of bullion. After several years of mining and smelting their ore in the Colorado Rockies, the Mexicans needed twenty-six burros to carry all the gold ingots they had accumulated. Loading their other belongings into heavy ox carts, they undertook a long journey to New Orleans, where they intended to book passage to some location on Mexico's east coast.

Sometime in the late spring of 1849, the Mexicans arrived in Santa Fe, New Mexico, to purchase supplies. After spending nearly a week in that city preparing equipment and material for the long trek across the prairie, the slow-moving pack train, accompanied by nearly twenty men, headed eastward. After crossing the Texas Panhandle, the party was negotiating the hilly grasslands in what is now Roger Mills County, Oklahoma, when disaster struck.

As the long pack train crested a low hill on the prairie, one of the riders at the rear of the caravan yelled a warning—Indians were approaching from the north. Ill-prepared for such an attack, the Mexicans' first impulse was to flee. Unable to goad the oxen into a gallop, they simply abandoned the heavy carts and concentrated on herding the ingot-laden burros to some defensible location.

Descending the low hill, one of the leaders spotted a shallow ravine not far away with a stream of water running through it. At one point along its course, the stream meandered in a nearly circular oxbow route around a slightly elevated sandy neck. Believing such a location offered some element of safety, the Mexicans whipped the burros toward it.

Seconds after arriving at their chosen location, the Mexicans dismounted and faced the oncoming attack. While most of them fired their seldom-used flintlocks at the charging Indians, others tried to maintain control of the frightened horses and burros.

Mistakenly, the Mexicans believed the Indians were after the gold they carried, unaware that the Indians cared little or nothing for the precious metal except for making occasional ornaments. When night fell, the Indians, unwilling to fight in the dark, retreated a short distance away from the battleground and made camp. When they were certain they were not being watched, the Mexicans decided to bury the gold on the island, leave the mules to distract the Indians, and effect an escape, intending to return someday to retrieve the ingots. For the next hour, the only sound that could be heard in the night was the scraping of shovels. When all of the gold was underground, the burros were turned loose, and the Mexicans rode away toward the southeast.

Precisely at dawn, the Indians arrived where the Mexicans had camped and discovered that they had fled. Quickly picking up their trail, the mounted warriors set out in pursuit, eventually overtaking the party and killing every member.

The fortune in gold ingots, estimated to be worth millions, lay buried on a sandy neck of land almost surrounded by a bend in a tiny stream on the Oklahoma prairie. It remained there for many years; its location completely unknown to anyone.

In 1890, an Indian attempted to pay for some goods at the Cheyenne-Arapaho Agency Trading Post on the Washita River with a curious-looking gold bar. The ingot, crudely smelted and at least ninety percent pure, was marked with a cross, a typical Spanish symbol often applied to gold and silver bars. The trading post's proprietor, instantly recognizing the gold for what it was, asked the Indian where he had obtained it.

The Indian, a Comanche, said he had dug it up on a small island in White Shield Creek. He explained that from time to time when he needed to make purchases, he went to the island and dug up one of the gold bars that the white men liked. He also stated there were hundreds more buried at the location, having been left there years earlier by some Mexicans who were massacred by a war party, which his grandfather had led. As the proprietor continued his questioning, the Indian grew suspicious, paid for his goods, and hastily departed. He was never seen again.

Accompanied by several friends, the trading post operator traveled to Carpenter Town, a tiny settlement about ten miles northeast of Elk City and close to White Shield Creek. On a nearby ridge, they found the remains of two or three ox carts and some rusted bridle bits and trace fittings. Just to the east was the creek, and, in plain view, what he described as a "gooseneck

120

curve" in the stream almost completely surrounding a body of land, making it appear like an island. After excavating a few holes on the "island," the men were unable to find anything, quickly became discouraged, and returned to the agency.

Since that time, only one concentrated effort has been initiated to try and find the gold ingots buried in the ravine gorged by White Shield Creek. An interested and persistent researcher, after studying all the information he could find concerning the buried Mexican gold, confided in several close friends that he believed he could locate it.

Using topographic maps published by the United States Geological Survey, the researcher studied the area thoroughly. He even sketched in the location of what he believed would have been a logical route through the area used by the Mexicans more than one hundred years earlier. He discerned what he believed to be the low ridge where they first saw the attacking Indians. According to his map, White Shield Creek was located just a few hundred yards east of this low ridge. In fact, the topographic map even indicated a part of the creek that curved around a neck of land into a nearly complete circle.

In a letter he composed to his wife, the researcher told about arriving in the area, climbing the low ridge, and, from his vantage point, spotting the curve in the stream. Just beyond the stream, he wrote, was an old railroad bed oriented in a north-south direction, and just to the east of that was State Highway 34. After arriving on the neck of land located within the curve of the stream, he claimed in his letter that, at last, he had found the long-buried gold ingots and that they were less than a mile from the highway. He further related that he intended to travel immediately to Elk City, rent a truck, and return to the site to recover the gold.

At Elk City, the researcher purchased a stamp and mailed the letter, rented a commercial van with heavy duty suspension, and checked into a cheap motel for the night. On the following morning, he drove north along Highway 34 toward a point where he intended to park the van while he recovered the ingots. At precisely 9:45 A.M., he was killed in a head-on collision with a pickup truck pulling a four-horse trailer.

Two days later, his wife received the letter. In spite of the directions contained in the letter, the widow never undertook to look for the treasure, a fortune in gold ingots that still lie buried today.

Cimarron County Gold Cache

The buried gold cache along White Shield Creek in Roger Mills County, Oklahoma, is not the only major lost treasure in western Oklahoma. About one hundred and forty miles to the northwest in Cimarron County in the state's Panhandle region lies yet another incredible fortune in hidden gold ingots. In the case of the Cimarron County treasure, however, the principals were Frenchmen instead of Mexicans, and they buried nearly four thousand pounds of gold.

During the late August heat in 1804, six large, creaky ox carts pulled by trail-weary and underfed oxen followed the route of what would eventually be known as the Santa Fe Trail. Seven Frenchmen, a Mexican guide, and about a dozen Indian slaves comprised the party and, after riding and walking since dawn, all looked forward to stopping for the night.

The group's leader, however, encouraged them onward at a pace that was debilitating for both men and animals. As he ordered his charges along the trail, he sat high in the saddle and constantly scanned the horizons, ever alert for any sign of Indians or bandits. His concentration was broken only occasionally when he felt it necessary to lash one of the Indian slaves to greater speeds.

The leader, a domineering man named Lafarge, was a native of France with a troubled past. Several years earlier, LaFarge was admitted to the priesthood in his native country and was soon afterward assigned to Mexico in the New World. Though many pertinent historical facts have been lost, it is known that LaFarge was convicted of killing a man and was subsequently relieved of his appointment. After a trial, he was sent to prison where he languished for several years.

Eventually, LaFarge was released, but he continued to assume the role of a holy man by wearing the robe and hood of a Catholic friar. After traveling for several years throughout northern Mexico, LaFarge crossed the Rio Grande and wandered from settlement to settlement, using his disguise to great advantage to procure food and lodging from unsuspecting residents. The imposter even performed baptisms and weddings.

The ex-priest soon became friends with six other Frenchmen he met at a small settlement in central New Mexico, and together the group journeyed northward to Taos where they became involved in a mining operation along several of the small mountain streams found in the vicinity.

None of the Frenchmen had any mining experience whatsoever and they soon became frustrated with the hard work that yielded only small amounts of gold from the streams. All around them, other miners were panning large quantities of nuggets, and the Frenchmen soon decided it would be easier to steal the gold from their neighbors than to continue to pan for their own. Over a period of about three months, the seven men systematically robbed and killed twenty-two miners and, in the process, accumulated several hundred pounds of gold.

As the quantity of stolen gold grew heavier, it became very difficult moving it from place to place. Because of the increasing danger of being discovered at their depredations, the Frenchmen decided it was time to leave the area. LaFarge hired Jose Lopat, a Mexican, to smelt the gold and form it into ingots for easy transportation. After Lopat molded a total of five hundred bars, LaFarge decided it would be prudent for the Frenchmen to pack the gold, travel to New Orleans, and charter passage on a ship that would take them back to their homeland where they could live like kings with their new-found wealth. Learning that Lopat was familiar with the Great Plains east of the mountain range, LaFarge employed him as a guide.

After purchasing provisions for the pack train at Santa Fe, the group departed eastward along a well-traveled trail that bisected the prairie. One day, as the party labored across a stretch of open prairie in what is now Cimarron County, Oklahoma, Lopat rode up to the ever-vigilant LaFarge and informed him of the location of a fresh-water spring a short distance away, and, as it was nearing sundown, the Mexican suggested it would be a good place to camp for the night. As they spoke, both LaFarge and Lopat noted a long, low mountain located a short distance to the north.

When the weary party finally arrived at the spring, they found four trappers already camped there. As the Frenchmen approached, the trappers welcomed them and invited the newcomers to share dinner. During conversation among the men that evening, LaFarge learned from the trappers that New Orleans no longer belonged to France and that it had been sold to the United States. The ex-priest grew concerned that the new government might not allow him to ship the gold ingots out of the country and might, in fact, even confiscate the treasure. Secretly, LaFarge confided these concerns to his fellow countrymen and, moving away from the trappers, discussed their predicament. It was eventually decided that two of the Frenchmen would travel to New Orleans and make arrangements for a ship to rendezvous with them at some specified date somewhere along the coast, far from scrutiny by the United States agents.

On the following morning, the Frenchmen selected for the task departed for New Orleans while LaFarge and the others prepared for the long stay at the spring. It was estimated that it would take the men three and a half months to make the round trip, so LaFarge ordered the Indians to construct several dugouts and rock dwellings to shelter them against the approaching winter.

By December's end, the two Frenchmen had not returned and LaFarge grew concerned. He finally concluded the best course of action was to bury the gold ingots near the spring and, along with his countrymen, travel to New Orleans, make arrangements to sail to France, and then return for the treasure. He sent Lopat and the Indians back to Santa Fe and, once they were out of sight, supervised the excavations of several deep holes into which the ingots were placed.

After returning to Santa Fe, Lopat learned about LaFarge's criminal past. Being quite literate, he wrote a description of LaFarge along with his own account of aiding the Frenchmen in transporting the gold ingots as far as the spring. When Lopat finished his manuscript, he placed it in the back of his Bible, and it is from this handwritten chronicle by Jose Lopat that researchers have learned much of what they know about LaFarge and his gold.

Nearly a year passed, and one day Lopat was surprised to encounter LaFarge, robed and hooded, walking down a Santa Fe street. LaFarge told the Mexican that after burying the gold ingots at the spring, the others were massacred by Indians and that only he escaped. He also stated he was the only one left alive who knew the location of the buried gold but was afraid to venture into Indian country. He told Lopat that he would wait for spring, gather a large party of armed men, and return to retrieve the gold. LaFarge asked Lopat to be a member of that expedition.

Lopat was distrustful of the ex-priest and suspected that he might have actually killed the others. The Mexican was also concerned that LaFarge might also kill him once he helped dig up the gold bars. He told the Frenchman he would think about it.

While Lopat talked to LaFarge, two miners came forth and identified the Frenchman as a member of the group that raided the gold camps of their companions, killing several, and making off with a hard-earned store of nuggets. A mob soon formed, and it ran through the streets of Santa Fe searching for the outlaw priest. LaFarge escaped for a time by hiding under some goods piled high in an ox cart, but he was soon discovered, dragged several miles out of town, and executed.

The knowledge of the precise location of the cached gold ingots was buried with LaFarge. Based on what the Frenchman told him, Lopat believed he could find the treasure and began to make arrangements to travel to the spring.

Lopat found the spring again without difficulty but discovered no clues that anything had ever been buried in the area. After digging a few holes and finding nothing, the Mexican grew discouraged, returned to Santa Fe, and never again concerned himself with the buried treasure.

During the next few decades, the story of LaFarge's buried ingots was on the lips of many, but no evidence exists that any organized attempt was made to find the gold. Then, in 1870, a series of strange stone markers were discovered in the vicinity of the Santa Fe Trail. These markers consisted of huge rocks rolled into place to form a "V" and were found located between five and ten miles apart. The point of the "V" was always oriented in the direction of the next marker. These odd directional-markers were found in a somewhat regular pattern from the town of Santa Fe, New Mexico, to the settlement of Las Vegas, nearly fifty miles to the east. Beyond Las Vegas, however, searchers were unable to locate any others. Several more years passed, and more of the stone markers were eventually discovered along the old road to Clayton, New Mexico, in the northeastern part of the state and near the tip of the Oklahoma panhandle—the trail that was taken by LaFarge and his party.

In 1900, a rancher named Ryan, along with two young ranch hands, was driving a herd of recently purchased horses from Clayton to his ranch in Cimarron County. One evening, as Ryan was setting up a night camp along a stretch of prairie, several of his new horses broke away from the main herd and escaped out onto the plains. Leaving his helpers in charge of the remaining animals, Ryan rode out the next morning to retrieve his lost livestock.

After several hours of searching for his ponies, Ryan stopped to rest, and as he sat in the shade of a tree smoking a cigarette he spotted another one of the strange stone markings. It consisted of large rocks like all the others and was again in the shape of a "V." Ryan, familiar with the legend of the lost gold ingots of LaFarge, was certain these man-made rock formations pointed the way to the treasure.

Over the next two years, Ryan searched for and found several more of the stone markers, all of which eventually led him to a spring in Cimarron County. Area residents knew the water hole as Flagg Springs, and Ryan believed it was the place where LaFarge and his party camped and buried the gold. For several years, the rancher excavated holes in the region but, like Lopat years before him, was never able to find any trace of the treasure.

Ryan's great nephew, Cy Strong, worked on a ranch in the county near Sugar Loaf Mountain. Strong had also studied the tale of LaFarge's buried treasure over the years and was convinced that Sugar Loaf was the long, low mountain seen by the Frenchman and Lopat just before setting up camp at Flagg Springs. A short distance from the springs, Strong found evidence of a very old dugout along with several adobe bricks and flat rocks that apparently comprised parts of several crude dwellings, most likely the shelters LaFarge had constructed. In addition, several pieces of rotted ox cart wheels were found nearby. Strong, like Ryan, excavated several sites near the spring but was unable to uncover any gold.

The evidence that Flagg Springs is the site at which LaFarge and his party buried the five hundred gold ingots is compelling, but the fact that numerous excavations in the area have been conducted with nothing of importance being recovered is rather puzzling. Several treasure hunters who have visited Flagg Springs and have seen the weathered shelters and pieces of ox carts are convinced beyond a doubt that the treasure was cached in the vicinity. Many believe it may have been buried as much as a hundred or more yards away because LaFarge, being unusually perceptive and canny, may have assumed that anyone searching for the gold would automatically think it was buried next to the spring. The researchers claim LaFarge transported it a specified distance and direction from the spring and interred it. After LaFarge's companions were killed, either by his hand or by Indians, he became the only person alive who knew the precise location.

The gold is there, claim scholars and historians, but no one knows exactly where. Since the turn of the century, untold numbers of treasure hunters have arrived at Flagg Springs to test their luck with the lost gold ingots. Some carry maps, many bring metal detectors, but thus far the Frenchman's fortune has eluded the searchers.

SOUTH DAKOTA

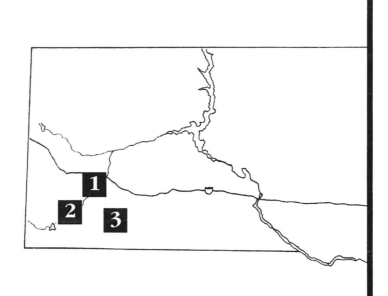

1. The *Monitor's* Stolen Fortune
2. The Central City Gold Shipment
3. A Hefty Gold Bar Robbery

The *Monitor's* Stolen Fortune

John Miner was the superintendent of the stage station in Canyon Springs, Wyoming, which served the Cheyenne-Black Hills Stage, Mail, and Express Line. Miner and two other men were responsible for maintaining spare horses, preparing meals for the stagecoach driver and its occupants, and otherwise managing the property that consisted of a single log building, a tack shed, and two horse corrals.

On the afternoon of September 26, 1878, Miner had just watered the horses and was returning to the main building when two strangers arrived on horseback. Waving at Miner, they dismounted and asked for a drink of water, and as Miner pointed toward the well, both men drew pistols and ordered the station manager to raise his hands. At a signal, three more horsemen rode into the yard from behind the concealment of a nearby grove of trees.

As one of the men marched Miner into the log building at gunpoint, the others tied the horses behind the station and followed. As Miner and his two helpers were securely bound and gagged, it became obvious to the station manager that these newcomers intended to rob the afternoon stage that would be arriving in about two hours.

Charles Carey, sometimes known as Jim Carey, led the outlaws on their pillaging adventures. Carey was only twenty-one years old, tall, well-built, and with a handsome face garnished by a light brown moustache. He was known to have been educated, had once worked a gold mining claim in Wyoming, and had a reputation for being fearless. Carey was accompanied by a less attractive band of ruffians—Thomas Goodale, Frank McBride, Al Spear, and another man known only as Red Cloud. Red Cloud was clearly not an Indian, and at least one historical reference indicates his real name was actually Andy Gough, a surly, reclusive individual who acquired his nickname as a result of having worked at the Red Cloud Indian Agency months earlier.

Miner and the two other station attendants were placed against the wall at one end of the log building. Carey instructed them to remain silent or they would be shot.

As the sun lowered on the western horizon, the stagecoach was heard approaching from the northeast along Deadwood Road. The coach was unlike any other. Lined with steel and having no windows, only gun ports, it was designed to carry a large cargo of currency, ore, and bullion and be easily defensible in the event of an attack from robbers. On this day, the *Monitor*, as it was called, carried seven hundred pounds of gold bullion, a shipment from the Homestead Mining Company, along with $3,500 in cash and nearly $30,000 worth of jewelry.

As driver Gene Barnett pulled the ponderous and heavy *Monitor* into the yard and up to the front of the station, he called out to Miner. Receiving no reply, he stood and looked about as guard Galen Hill laid his rifle on the wooden spring seat and jumped to the ground to place chocks under the front wheels. Just after securing the first chock, a shot rang out from the station and Hill fell with a severe wound in his left arm. Rising to a seated position, the guard pulled his revolver from the holster and, spotting the gunman silhouetted in the front window of the station, fired three shots, mortally wounding McBride. As McBride fell, Spear appeared at the same window, aimed a rifle at Hill, and shot him in the chest. Though seriously wounded, Hill returned fire, striking his assailant. Out of bullets, Hill tossed his revolver away and scrambled to relative safety behind the wheels of the stagecoach.

When the shooting started, Eugene Smith, one of three other guards inside the coach, leaped out and began shooting toward the open window of the station. As he paused to reload his pistol, Smith was hit in the leg by one of the outlaws and crumpled to the ground. The two other guards, Scott Davis and Hugh Campbell, exited from the opposite side of the coach and ran toward the corrals across the road. Campbell was struck in the back and killed instantly; Davis escaped into the same grove of trees where the outlaws had hidden earlier that afternoon.

As the shooting died down, driver Barnett simply held his hands above his head and surrendered without ever drawing his gun. Carey, Goodale, and Spear tied him and the two wounded guards, Hill and Smith, to the wagon wheels. Red Cloud carried the dying McBride out of the station and into the waning sunlight, laid him on the ground, and ministered to him as the others looted the *Monitor*.

As the outlaws loaded the gold, currency, and jewelry onto several of the horses they liberated from the corral, guard Davis fled along a ravine, determined to make his way to Ben Eager's ranch, about seven miles away, and report the holdup.

After law enforcement officials and the stage line had been informed of the robbery, several posses were formed, all of which convened at the Canyon Springs Stage Station. After untying the employees, W. M. Ward, a representative for the stage line, arrived. After gathering facts relative to the holdup, Ward offered a $2,500 reward for the capture of the bandits and the return of the stage's contents. In addition, the stage company official promised a percentage of any of the recovered cargo. When word of the reward spread around the countryside, as many as fifteen separate posses combed the region searching for the outlaws.

For two days, armed men—law officers as well as vigilantes—fanned out into parts of Wyoming and South Dakota. Travelers were stopped and questioned and wagons searched, but the posse members encountered no sign of the robbers or any of the robbery loot. Ward, accompanied by a small group of armed riders, found some wagon tracks heading toward the southeast and decided to follow them.

Then, late on the afternoon of the second day, Ward encountered a rancher near Harney Peak in South Dakota's Black Hills who said he had sold one of his wagons to a group of rough-looking men earlier that morning. His description of the purchasers matched that of the robbers and the rancher stated that two of the men were badly wounded and that one appeared near the brink of death.

On the third day following the robbery, another posse arrived at the Horsehead Crossing Stage Station and received encouraging news from the station manager, George Boland. Boland told the trackers that a heavily loaded canvas-covered wagon, accompanied by three men, had ridden up to the station that morning. One of the men was unconscious and bleeding badly from a chest wound. The newcomers asked Boland if he would make arrangements to get the wounded man to a doctor. They handed him one hundred dollars in cash, unloaded McBride from the wagon, and sped away. Only moments after the men departed, McBride died and the station manager buried him on a low hill behind the building.

Ward was notified and hours later, after arriving at the Horsehead Crossing Station, set out after the outlaws. Though he was tracking a large, slow-moving wagon transporting an extremely heavy load, he somehow lost the trail.

Carey, Goodale, Spear, and Red Cloud continued to drive the wagon southeastward toward Table Mountain. Spear's wound was much worse than originally believed, and he often cried out in pain as the wagon bounced over the uneven roads. As the day wore on, Spear gradually lost consciousness. It was a tired, hungry, and haggard group of men that finally arrived at a secluded canyon on the northwest side of Table Mountain, not far from the present-day Badlands National Monument.

The next morning, Carey suggested that they temporarily bury the wagon load of loot in the canyon. It would make sense, he told his companions, to separate and leave the country for about a year before returning to recover the fortune in gold and jewelry. By then, he claimed, interest in the robbery would have died down and they would likely be able to move about the region without attracting suspicion.

While Carey, Goodale, and Red Cloud excavated a large hole, Al Spear died from his wound. His body, wrapped in an old blanket, was placed in a second hole next to the buried treasure.

The following morning, Carey and Red Cloud rode west, intending to return to Wyoming and seek work on a ranch. Goodale returned to his hometown of Atlantic, a small town in southwestern Iowa. Unknown to Carey and Red Cloud, Goodale had slipped one of the heavy gold bars along with several items of jewelry from the cache and into his saddlebags.

Three days later, Carey and Red Cloud were fixing breakfast over a low fire near the South Dakota-Wyoming border when they were startled by the arrival of a large group of men on horseback. Carey's heart sank as he recognized the leader of the posse—it was the stagecoach guard Scott Davis!

Davis quickly identified Carey and Red Cloud, and within the hour, the two outlaws were dead, both of them hung from a limb of the large oak tree that shaded their quiet campsite.

Goodale, arriving in Atlantic several days later, moved in with his parents and took a job with his father, the owner of the town's bank. Somewhat impressed with his adventures as an outlaw, the young Goodale, twenty-two, proudly displayed the gold bar taken from the stagecoach robbery. Goodale's father, believing his son had acquired the gold honestly, even permitted it to be displayed in the front window of the bank.

Meanwhile Ward, a determined and tenacious investigator, followed a series of vague clues and, several weeks later, arrived in Atlantic. Casually strolling the town's main street one morning, Ward was passing time by looking in shop windows when he noticed a gold bar prominently displayed in the front window of the bank. There, etched on the $4,300 ingot, was the inscription "Homestake No. 12," leaving little doubt that it had been taken in the Monitor's robbery.

Two days later, young Goodale was arrested, and among his belongings Ward found a gold watch and several diamond rings, later identified as items taken during the holdup.

Under questioning, Goodale, now very frightened and showing none of his earlier bluster, admitted his part in the robbery. He told about the deaths of McBride and Spear and related in detail the burial of the gold and jewelry near Table Mountain.

Ward intended to return to Table Mountain with his prisoner and have him provide directions to the buried loot, but during the trip to the jail at Cheyenne, Wyoming, Goodale managed to escape while the train was stopped at Lone Tree, Nebraska. The young outlaw was never seen again, and it was believed he fled to Mexico. Goodale was the only living person who knew the exact location of the buried treasure cache.

Before Ward was able to journey to Table Mountain, a man named Whitfield, a member of one of the original posses, had learned of the cache in that area. Entering one of the canyons that bisects the mountain, he discovered the abandoned wagon, the remains of a campfire, and some discarded clothes, all bloodied and stiff. Nearby he located the grave of Al Spears but could not find the cache of gold and jewels.

Returning to the pile of old clothes, Whitfield decided to search the pockets and discovered a gold bar wrapped in a pair of torn overalls. He returned the ingot, valued at $3,200, to the stage line and received a reward of $1,100.

A few days later, Ward, accompanied by several men, arrived at Table Mountain. He located the wagon and campsite of the outlaws, but, like Whitfield, was unable to find the cache. After several more trips to the canyon, Ward eventually gave up the search and officially closed the case as far as the stage line was concerned.

Interest in the buried fortune gradually waned with the passing years, but in 1933 an amazing discovery rekindled public interest in the forty-five-year-old robbery of the *Monitor* and the unrecovered gold. Terry O'Neill, a South Dakota rancher, was searching for a lost calf on horseback near the Badlands when approaching darkness forced him to find a campsite for the night. Staking his horse out near what he identified as Sheep Mountain, O'Neill was gathering wood for a fire when he noticed a rectangular object poking up from a portion of the ground that had been eroded away by runoff from a thunderstorm of the previous day. Picking up the item, O'Neill was surprised at its relatively heavy weight. After cleaning the dirt from the surface, he noticed the inscription "Homestake Mining Company" on the top and, on closer inspection, realized he was holding a gold ingot. Believing it was the only ingot buried at this site, O'Neill did not consider searching any further.

After O'Neill reported his discovery, investigators who questioned him learned that what he identified as Sheep Mountain may actually have been Table Mountain. Sheep Mountain lies approximately a mile north of Table Mountain.

From the entire shipment of gold bars, jewelry, and cash taken in the holdup of the *Monitor*, only two of the ingots, a watch, and a few rings have been recovered. Somewhere in a Table Mountain canyon, the remainder of this huge treasure lies buried, its location still uncertain to this day.

The Central City Gold Shipment

Central City, South Dakota, like many towns associated with the gold rush of the last century, was a lively, growing center of commercial activity. Miners and engineers from the Black Hills flocked into town to spend money on supplies and entertainment, and during the latter part of the nineteenth century, Central City boasted a population of approximately ten thousand people.

A town as large and varied as Central City responded to the needs of its citizens with schools, stores, taverns, theaters, banks, and even social clubs. At one time, the city was home to four newspapers, several smelters, and sixteen stamp mills for crushing ore.

In 1884, a group of investors founded the Dakota Bullion Exchange. Great profits could be made, they determined, from assaying and purchasing gold in exchange for currency that the miners could more easily and appropriately use in the city's retail establishments. When the Exchange accumulated a sufficient amount of gold, it was smelted into ingots and transported across the mountains through Deadwood and on to Fort Meade, a military post.

On the morning of March 5, 1884, Exchange employees were preparing a shipment of fifty gold ingots. The bars were loaded onto a wagon, tied down, and covered with a canvas tarp. Around nine o'clock, as an employee secured four horses to the trace chains, the driver and armed guard stood by the loaded wagon smoking cigarettes while waiting for the arrival of an armed military escort of twenty soldiers.

Previous shipments from Central City to Fort Meade had always been completed efficiently and without threat, and the soldiers assigned to guard the shipment treated the assignment rather casually. In fact, as the two men lit another cigarette, the soldiers were ordering drinks in a tavern about three blocks away.

During the previous three weeks, three prospectors—Elmer Maxwell, Clark Simmons, and Harry Woode—slept in a tool shed behind the Exchange. The men had no luck searching for gold in the nearby hills and had been reduced to begging for handouts on the streets of Central City. On this particular morning, the three men watched the loading of the fifty gold ingots onto the wagon and pondered this great fortune that was to be transported out of town. They also considered the possibility of stealing it.

After finishing his second cigarette, the guard walked down to the tavern and informed the escort that the wagon was loaded and ready to depart. As the driver leaned against the wagon, Woode came from behind the building carrying an iron rod. The driver suspected nothing as Woode approached, smiling and waving. Suddenly, the miner swung the piece of iron around, striking the driver in the head and knocking him unconscious to the ground.

The driver had no sooner hit the ground when Maxwell and Simmons raced from behind the same building to help Woode carry his limp form to a shallow ravine about thirty yards away. The three men then climbed onto the wagon and rode casually out of town, waving and smiling at citizens as they went.

After traveling about fifteen miles along the winding road between Central City and Deadwood at a consistent gallop, the horses began to show signs of fatigue. Simmons, concerned for the animals' welfare, suggested finding a spot to camp for the night and allow the horses some rest. Turning left off the trail and into a forested canyon, the hijackers unhitched the team and let the horses graze. While Woode built a small fire, Simmons and Maxwell hunted for rabbits.

The next morning, one of the horses was so lame it was clearly unfit to pull the heavily loaded wagon. Concerned that only three horses might not be enough, the men decided to bury the gold at this site, hide the wagon, and ride the three good horses to Deadwood. After obtaining a team of fresh horses, they planned to return to the canyon and retrieve the gold ingots. Each of the men took one ingot and buried the remaining forty-seven near their campsite.

By this time, the army escort, along with several Central City citizens, were combing the countryside in search of the bandits.

Maxwell, Simmons, and Woode spent nearly a week in Deadwood, but had no luck whatsoever finding anyone who would sell them a team of horses. They decided to return to the canyon, looking for horses to steal along the way. Riding southeastward from Deadwood, the trio encountered a mounted platoon of soldiers who, recognizing the outlaws, pursued and finally captured them. The bandits were taken to Fort Meade and placed in the stockade. Though each was interrogated extensively, none revealed the location of the buried gold ingots. The three men were tried, convicted, and sentenced to life in prison for the robbery. Undeterred by the heavy penalty, the three immediately began planning an escape and a return to the canyon to recover the gold.

But it was not to happen. In the fourth month of their incarceration, Woode was shot and killed during an escape attempt. Within the year, Simmons became ill with tuberculosis and declined in health until he was little more than an invalid. He was confined to a bed for nearly three years before he died.

Maxwell, the only man living who knew the location of the forty-seven gold bars, was eventually transferred to an army prison in Pennsylvania. After only a week at this new location, Maxwell was stabbed by his cellmate and died the following day.

Though many people searched for the missing gold bars for several years following the robbery, no one had the remotest idea where they could have been hidden. Eventually the story of the hijacking and subsequent caching of the fortune in gold bullion became a dim memory for all but a few residents of this part of South Dakota.

Then one day in 1902, a hunter arrived at Rapid City and checked into a hotel. Dining with several companions that same evening in the hotel restaurant, he told about finding the remains of an old freight wagon while hunting for bear in a remote canyon between Central City and Deadwood. One of the wagon planks, he said, was branded with the name Dakota Bullion Exchange.

At a nearby table, a reporter for one of the Rapid City newspapers overheard the comment and, being familiar with the story of the lost gold, sought an audience with the hunter.

Later that evening, the reporter told the hunter the story of the hijacked gold and suggested that the wagon's discovery was the only substantial evidence pointing to a location where it was likely buried. Intrigued, the hunter agreed to take the reporter out to the canyon the next day.

That night, however, the hunter developed severe stomach pains, crawled down the stairs to the front desk, and begged to be taken to a doctor. By the time he was carried to the office of a nearby physician, he was dead, and with his passing went the only knowledge of the potential location of the lost forty-seven gold ingots.

A Hefty Gold Bar Robbery

Paul Wagner had lived in the Black Hills for three years, all of them spent working for the Wilson Freight Company. For fifteen dollars a month and permission to sleep in the livery, Wagner hauled supplies to the mines, ore to the stamp mills, and refined ingots to overland transport companies specializing in long hauls to the federal mint at Denver.

A native of the Pennsylvania Appalachians, Wagner migrated to the Black Hills with hopes of striking it rich in the gold fields, but like so many others who came here seeking their fortunes, he encountered little but hard luck. Penniless and hungry, he was eventually offered a job as a driver for the freight company, which he accepted with enthusiasm.

Wagner, a good driver and loyal employee, volunteered to make deliveries into the remotest regions of the mountain range, and he would offer to haul freight in bad weather when the other drivers demurred. In his spare time, he often groomed and fed the horses at the freight yard stables. Freight magnate Wilson found he could rely on Wagner more than he could any other employee.

While working for Wilson, Wagner often thought about the great wealth he sometimes transported in the back of his wagon. As he steered the team of horses down lonely trails, he occasionally dreamed of the things such wealth could provide: dining at fine restaurants in San Francisco and Denver, wearing expensive, tailored clothes, smoking imported cigars while gaming at the casinos. And women—Wagner often thought about women.

Wagner was tempted often, and many times he considered driving away with a wagonload of gold ingots or ore.

The visions of grandeur came and went, and Wagner sometimes felt very guilty for even considering such things. After all, he had a good job and a place to sleep. But still he wondered, and he continued to dream.

Around dawn one cloudy September morning, Wagner was summoned to Wilson's loading dock. On arriving, he was informed that he was to deliver two large gold ingots across town to the dock at Hermann Freight. There, he was to help load them onto a large, sturdy wagon with heavy suspension for the trip to Denver.

As Wagner visited with other Wilson Freight employees, driver Fred Smith steered his large four horse-drawn delivery wagon into the yard. The stout horses were blowing hard as Smith set the brakes and climbed down from the seat. Smith, who had worked for Wilson for nearly seven years, had been sent to the Royal Mining and Smelter Company deep in the Black Hills to pick up two five-hundred-pound gold ingots. When the driver yanked back the canvas tarp covering the two large gold bars lashed securely to the wagon bed, Wagner gazed in awe. Here indeed, he pondered, was a king's wealth. And what wonderful things such wealth could bring.

Smelting gold ore and shaping it into large ingots such as these, it was explained to Wagner, was a deterrent to bandits. Heretofore, highwaymen could easily hold up a freight wagon and escape with a large number of the smaller, standard-sized ingots that often weighed less than forty pounds apiece. Five-hundred-pound ingots, however, were too large and ponderous to be carried away on horseback.

As Smith, Wilson, and the others walked across the loading dock and into the freight office, Wagner remained transfixed by the two large ingots. When the door to the office slammed shut, Wagner decided on the spur of the moment to steal the gold and flee into the prairie, which stretched out for miles east of town.

Parked in front of the freight office was the wagon J.B. Wilson drove to work on that morning, a light spring wagon suitable for transporting two people and a small amount of freight. As Wagner looked at the businessman's wagon, an idea formed in his mind. Because Wilson only traveled a few hundred yards from his house to the office, the two horses that pulled the wagon and were still linked to the traces were relatively fresh, while the team of animals that pulled Smith's heavy wagon from the smelter were exhausted and hungry.

Grabbing the lead reins of Wilson's team, Wagner lead them over to the large cargo wagon. Positioning the back of the light wagon next to the rear of the cargo wagon, Wagner slid the heavy bars from one to the other and then covered them with the canvas tarp. As he labored, he kept a constant watch on the office door, fearful that Wilson or one of his other employees might emerge and detect the theft.

The light, almost frail, wagon strained, creaked, and sagged under the heavy load of the large ingots. Leaping onto the spring seat, Wagner lashed at the horses and fled down the main street of Rapid City and out onto the prairie to the east.

Wagner began to realize the folly of his decision to rob the Wilson Freight Company within minutes after riding past the city limits. Though they had only traveled about five miles, the horses, used to pulling light loads for short distances, were already tired and slowing down. Wagner began to fear they would grow lame and be unable to continue. The great weight of the two huge ingots was also placing incredible strain on the lightly constructed wagon, and each time the wagon bounced across some irregularity in the road, Wagner heard the sound of the thin, flimsy bed timbers cracking and snapping.

After covering about ten miles, Wagner scanned the horizon behind him and, perceiving no pursuit, slowed the tired horses to a walk. Peering under the canvas covering, he noted that several of the wagon planks now had small fractures, and the entire weight of the ingots was causing the bed to bow dramatically. Overhead, the clouds grew darker, threatening rain, and the wind increased its velocity, harshly whipping the prairie grasses back and forth.

As Wagner considered burying the ingots along the trail and returning for them later, disaster struck. Cresting on a low ridge on the prairie about a half-mile to his left, the driver spotted about thirty Indians strung out in a long row, slowly and deliberately advancing toward him.

Sioux! During the previous six months, several freight wagons had been attacked by Indians, residents of these plains for generations who resented being displaced from their sacred Black Hills by white intruders. Fearing for his life, Wagner, in a panic, lashed clumsily at the already exhausted horses, coaxing them on to speeds they were unable to achieve.

Glancing once again at the Indians, fear closed tightly around Wagner's chest as he saw them now in full gallop and rapidly gaining on the lone wagon. Deciding to quit the trail, Wagner steered the animals across the grassy prairie in the vain hope of eluding his attackers by hiding in a gully. The driver had never owned a gun in his life, but at this moment he would have traded both of the five-hundred-pound gold ingots for a rifle.

As the wagon bounced over prairie dog mounds and into ruts, the strain of the great weight of the gold on the fragile wagon bed became too great. Seconds later when the wagon crossed a shallow, dry creek bed, the middle planks in the bed snapped and the two ingots dropped heavily into the gravelly stream bottom, each making a dull thumping noise as it struck the ground.

Ten seconds later, one of the horses stepped into a prairie dog hole, breaking a leg and tumbling to the ground. The momentum caused the second horse to follow, and Wagner leaped from the wagon a split second before it flipped over.

Wagner, dazed from the fall with blood trickling down his face from striking a rock moments earlier, tried to rise from the ground and discovered he was surrounded by a horde of angry, painted, screaming Sioux. Seconds later, Paul Wagner lay dead upon the prairie grasses, pierced by at least fifty arrows and several lances. As the driver's blood crimsoned the yellowing autumn prairie grasses, small drops of rain began to fall from the densely overcast sky.

After finding nothing of value in the shattered wagon, the Indians cut the struggling horse from the trace, leaving the one with the broken leg where it lay, and quickly departed the area, each riding by the fallen driver and counting coup with club or lance. As the Sioux disappeared over the low ridge where they were first seen by Wagner, the skies opened up and released a downpour that continued uninterrupted for three days. As the heavy rain diluted and washed Wagner's blood into the porous prairie soil, the little creek where the two five-hundred-pound gold ingots began to fill with water, rising quickly from the rapid accumulation of surface runoff and surging downstream from the pull of gravity. Tiny particles of sand, silt, and clay carried by the rushing waters were trapped against the upstream-facing sides of the gold bars lying the creek bottom. Before the storm finally passed from the region, the bars would become completely covered by a thin layer of sedimentary debris.

Almost two hours passed from the time Wagner fled with the gold ingots until the theft was discovered. Initially, Wilson believed the driver simply delivered the bars to the Hermann Freight Yard, but when one of his employees checked on the delivery, the events of the robbery grew clear.

After the sheriff was alerted, a posse of some fifteen men was assembled, and as the low clouds grew and thickened overhead, they rode out of Rapid City, following the tracks of the spring wagon driven by Wagner.

When the posse had been on the trail for nearly an hour, the rains finally came. Because of the storm's intensity and the reduced visibility, the lawmen returned to town, determined to renew pursuit as soon as the weather cleared.

Three days later when the clouds thinned out and the sun finally emerged, the posse reassembled and struck out in search of Wagner and the stolen gold. As the lawmen rode along the trail about two hours later, one of the riders spotted buzzards circling an area on the prairie about a mile south of the trail. The sheriff sent one of the deputies to investigate, and several minutes later the arrow- and lance-riddled body of Wagner was discovered. The remains of the broken wagon and one dead horse were strewn nearby.

After examining the wagon, the sheriff accurately deduced that the great weight of the stolen ingots was responsible for its breakage. The sheriff considered that the two gold bars must lay somewhere between the main road and the place where Wagner's body was found because the Sioux cared nothing for such things and would have left them, if they had found them. The storm, however, had washed away any evidence of the route taken by the fleeing wagoner. Though an intensive search was conducted for the next six hours, the gold bars were not found. Time and again, the lawmen crossed the tiny creek, passing within only a few feet of the sediment-covered ingots.

When the sheriff reported the bars missing, the mine owners and freight companies were compensated for their loss by the insurance companies, and the matter was quickly forgotten.

Several years following the robbery of the five-hundred-pound gold ingots and Paul Wagner's death, a newspaper reporter was looking over some documents and papers that once belonged to the Wilson Freight Company. After Wilson died from a heart attack, the business, including wagons and livestock, were purchased by the Hermann Freight Company. As the reporter searched the papers looking for something of historical significance, he came across several references to Wagner's theft of the ingots.

After a story on the lost gold bars came out in the paper the following week, many Rapid City residents began searching the small stream beds east of town, all hoping to locate the fortune. Unfortunately, there were no references to which of the several trails Wagner elected to utilize for his escape, and the gold bars were never found.

In 1932, a South Dakota rancher was riding across his pasture checking on his cattle when he spotted a rectangular object projecting from a creek bottom he was crossing. Dismounting, the rancher pulled with great effort an extremely heavy piece of metal from the sands and gravel of the little wash. The dark, corroded appearance of the object caused him to deduce that it was a piece of lead discarded by railroad employees years earlier when they were laying track in the area so he left it where it lay.

In 1938, the rancher learned the story of the stolen gold ingots and realized the heavy object he had found in the creek bottom was one of them. Enthused at the possibility of becoming rich from recovering the gold bars, he returned to the region to relocate and recover them. Though he searched the prairie for days, he was never able to find the ingots.

Alternately exposed and covered by the sometimes sediment-laden creek waters, the two five-hundred-pound ingots are still laying in the bottom of the small ephemeral stream bed where they dropped, awaiting a chance discovery by some fortunate passerby.

Texas

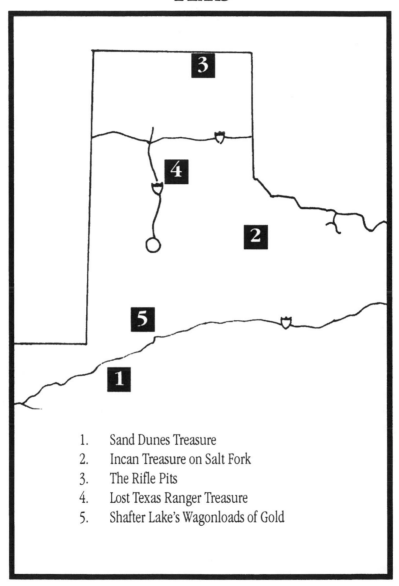

1. Sand Dunes Treasure
2. Incan Treasure on Salt Fork
3. The Rifle Pits
4. Lost Texas Ranger Treasure
5. Shafter Lake's Wagonloads of Gold

Sand Dunes Treasure

During the autumn of 1873, the wagon yard on the eastern outskirts of Yuma, Arizona, bustled with activity. Forty newly-purchased wagons were being readied for a long journey to Missouri, and dozens of families, most of Dutch descent, were making final preparations. Daniel Flake—the guide who would lead these eager travelers through the southwestern deserts, into the heartland of the growing nation and to the banks of the Mississippi River—watched silently as four hundred and seventy seven twenty-pound gold ingots were loaded into the wagons.

Several years earlier, these same families arrived in the California gold fields to seek their fortunes. Working as much as eighteen hours a day, seven days a week, these Dutch immigrants reaped fortunes from the gold ore they panned from the creek beds and mined from the solid rock of the Sierra Nevadas. The gold was accumulated and hoarded until such time as it was determined they had enough to fund the establishment of a farming community somewhere in the Mississippi River Valley, perhaps Missouri or Illinois.

When the elder leaders of the immigrants decided it was time, a portion of the gold was taken to Los Angeles where sturdy wagons and teams of fine horses and oxen were purchased for the long trip east. The remainder of the gold was smelted into twenty-pound ingots for easy loading and transportation. One by one, the families gradually abandoned their successful claims in the mountains and, over a period of weeks, joined the others at Yuma in a prearranged rendezvous.

When everyone was finally ready, Flake signaled the starting of the long wagon train on the eastbound journey out of the Yuma wagon yard and into the desert wilderness of southern Arizona.

Months passed. The travelers survived drought, floods, fierce sandstorms, horse-stealing Apaches, and washed-out trails. The forty wagons, along with their precious cargo, remained intact and were none the worse for wear. After fording the Pecos River near Horsehead Crossing early in spring 1874, Comanche Indians often followed the wagon train at a distance. When outriders attempted to approach the Indians, the Comanches turned their ponies and simply faded into the landscape. For several days, Flake, a veteran of many such wagon train expeditions, harbored an uncomfortable feeling about the Indians. Though he fought it, he could not shake a premonition of disaster that constantly intruded on his thoughts. In response, Flake doubled the guards and, though it was difficult, tried his best to increase the ten-to-fifteen-mile-per-day speed of the wagons. From the Pecos River, the train continued on a northeasterly course toward Missouri, rolling across the arid plains of west Texas.

Several days earlier, the travelers had filled their water barrels with the sediment-laden water they encountered in the Pecos River. The barrels were now nearly empty; their partial loads clearly audible as they sloshed with each forward jerk of the wagons. Flake, determined to locate a fresh-water spring before another day passed, sent scouts out ahead of the wagon train to search for one.

Late the following morning, two scouts rode up and informed Flake that a clear water spring was located several miles away in the middle of a cluster of sand dunes. As Flake guided the wagons toward the dunes, he spotted a line of Comanches on the southern horizon, armed warriors perched silent and still atop short, stout ponies. As Flake watched, more Indians arrived until the line of warriors extended for nearly a mile across the horizon. Flake estimated their number at several hundred.

About an hour later, the wagons entered a landscape quite different from what they had encountered thus far. Great white sand hills extended as far as the eye could see and ranged twenty to one hundred feet in height. The sand was so loosely consolidated in some places that horses and oxen sank up to eighteen inches with each step. The heavy wagons quickly slid into the soft sand and teams of men and animals struggled mightily to free them. While the immigrants were occupied with freeing the stuck wagons, Flake observed the Comanches walking their ponies closer and closer to the wagon train, a deliberate and unhurried pace that sent chills of terror up the spine of the wagon master. Before long, the Indians were close enough that Flake could see the hawk and eagle feathers attached to the warriors' braids and the manes, halters, and tails of the ponies. From the long, steel-pointed lances carried by many of the warriors, Flake saw more feathers moving in response to the desert breeze. Along with the feathers, other objects dangling from the weapons caught his attention, and it was several moments before the guide realized they were scalps.

The party eventually reached the spring, and as women and children hastened to fill the barrels with cool fresh water, Flake ordered the men to arrange the wagons into a defensive circle in the event of an Indian attack. Flake was unaware that the spring was a traditional water source and campsite for the Comanches during their long journeys into Mexico where they conducted raids—taking horses and captives.

As the late afternoon sun dropped low on the western horizon, Flake watched as the Comanches slowly encircled the immigrant encampment. Tension was high among the travelers as they prepared to settle in for the evening. A few moments before dark, the Indians quietly vanished.

During the night, several Dutch elders approached Flake and voiced concerns about the fortune in gold ingots they carried in the wagons. Despite assurances from the guide that the Comanches cared little or nothing for gold, the men insisted the ingots be removed from the wagons and buried until they were certain the Indians meant to do them no harm. Grudgingly, Flake assisted the men for the next several hours as the nearly five hundred gold ingots were buried in several dozen different locations within the circle of wagons.

As the first rays of morning sunlight broke across the land and illuminated the immigrant encampment, a lone Comanche on horseback, carrying a lance with a scalp festoon, rode to the top of a high dune just east of the awakening camp. Several of the travelers, bustling about and preparing for departure, kept a wary eye on the Indian. Presently, the Comanche raised his lance high above his head and within seconds was joined by hundreds of more riders, all armed with similar lances, bows and arrows, and wicked-looking war clubs. A few carried rifles. Flake stepped outside the perimeter of wagons and considered approaching the Indians for a talk when the silence of the early morning was shattered by a piercing war cry. Seconds later, the riders thundered down the dune toward the wagons, their high-pitched cries mingling with the screams of the frightened immigrants.

Before a sufficient number of the Dutchmen could locate their guns and before the women and children were able to attain relative safety in the beds of the wagons, the Comanches were upon them, slashing, shooting, cutting, stabbing, until, barely thirty minutes later, every member of the wagon train lay dead or dying.

As dozens of warriors commenced looting the wagons, others went from victim to victim, methodically taking scalps from men, women, and children alike. Before the sun was high in the heavens, the sandy battleground was littered not only with the bodies of the immigrants but also with unwanted items tossed from opened trunks. As the horses and oxen were cut from the traces and herded away, several braves set fire to the wagons.

With the newly acquired livestock added to the already large herd recently brought up from Mexico, the Comanches, wearing items of clothing taken from the dead, rode out of the sand dunes toward the north where they would join other warriors.

As the growing spring breeze began to stir the surface sand grains near the spring, forty wagons burned fiercely, smoke billowing high above the desert floor before the stronger winds at higher altitudes carried it away. More than a hundred bodies lay scattered among the ruined campsite. Many were naked, some were mutilated, and all were scalped. The porous sand under each corpse had efficiently absorbed the blood spilled by the victims, leaving only a light, pastel blotch of red on the surface. The buzzards, dozens of them, already circled just beyond the smoke's edge as the hot desert sun beat down upon the white sands.

Inside the burning circle of wagons, a great fortune in gold ingots lay buried, nearly ten thousand pounds of almost pure ore, which would have provided a new beginning for the dead immigrants.

Weeks passed, then months, then years, and the dunes, ever-shifting in response to the constant Texas winds, closed in on the debris of the battle. The once sturdy wagons were little more than piles of ash, though here and there a plank of a bed, a steel-rimmed wheel, a harness trace survived intact. Bones lay randomly scattered throughout the area; the flesh long since yielded to scavenging buzzards and coyotes.

Except for an occasional passing Indian, travelers avoided the sand dunes for the next twenty-nine years. Then, in 1903, an expedition led by retired Army Colonel Arthur Hayes entered the sandhills, located in what is now Winkler County. Hayes, a prominent judge in the region, occasionally organized such expeditions to explore and evaluate land that might someday prove to be suitable for grazing livestock. As the party, directed by scout Robert Brown, approached Willow Springs near a location called Flag Point, several pieces of timber, wagon wheels, and various metal fastenings could be seen sticking up through a layer of sand. The men searched and examined the area for several hours, finding dozens of human skeletons, some with skulls that had obviously been crushed by heavy instruments. Many bones had arrowheads embedded in the matrix. As Hayes pieced together the bits of evidence at the scene, it gradually became clear to him that they had stumbled upon the remains of a massacred wagon train.

Colonel Hayes became obsessed with this discovery. For the next several years, he attempted to learn the identity of the massacred party, its point of origin, and its intended destination. Hayes died before he learned the answers, but years later, others who researched the massacre site discovered an old clipping from an 1873 edition of a Yuma newspaper. From this, the investigators learned of the rich cargo of gold ingots transported by the unfortunate wagon train.

Spurred by the likelihood that a great fortune in gold lay just under the sand within the ring of burned and buried wagon train debris, researchers returned to the dunes only to discover that the shifting desert sands had once again covered up the site, perhaps to depths exceeding three feet. During the years that had passed since the massacre, the remains had been scattered, rotted, blown away, or covered up until the exact location of the immigrant campsite was no longer apparent.

After the story of the massacre and the buried gold became well known, hundreds of others have attempted to locate the site over the years. From time to time, individuals have found artifacts from the train, but to date the gold has not been located. Today, these sandhills comprise Monahans Sandhills State Park, owned and managed by the state of Texas. By law, treasure hunting is forbidden within the boundaries of the park, but 477 gold ingots, today worth between three and four million dollars, still lure treasure hunters and adventurers from deep below the white shifting sands.

Incan Treasure on Salt Folk

One of the most incredible buried treasure tales ever associated with the Great Plains is the legendary Inca hoard apparently buried near the Salt Fork of the Brazos River in Stonewall County, Texas. The treasure, estimated by experts to be worth between $50 and $100 million reportedly consists of the equivalent of forty mule loads of gold and silver bullion, jewelry, emeralds as large as goose eggs, and several jewel-encrusted golden Incan icons. Researchers also suggest that one of the first Bibles ever to arrive in the western hemisphere may be in the cache.

While this lost treasure's presumed location is in the arid Panhandle region of the Texas plains, the origin of the tale occurred more than four hundred and fifty years ago and three thousand miles away in the mountains of Peru, South America, the homeland of the once-powerful Incas.

In February 1531, the Spanish soldier and explorer Francisco Pizarro arrived with a convoy of three galleons at the port of Callao on the Peruvian Coast. A contingent of soldiers, a priest, and twenty-seven horses accompanied Pizarro. Under orders from the Spanish monarch, Pizarro was to explore the country in search of precious metals. If any was found, he would confiscate them and ship them back to Spain.

Pizarro was well known as a soldier. Years earlier, he had established a reputation for ruthlessness during several military campaigns, and the king of Spain believed him to be well-suited for conquering portions of South America and seizing the continent's wealth.

After spending several months making plans and stocking up on supplies and equipment, Pizarro led a force of one hundred and seventy bearded, armor-clad, fighting Spanish soldiers into the forested foothills of southeastern Peru. Pizarro and his men attacked and destroyed every village they encountered, indiscriminately killing men, women, and children, and seizing food and livestock. After several weeks of working their way across the rugged countryside, the Spaniards inflicted inhumane misery but failed to locate any significant amounts of precious metals.

Eventually, the Spaniards arrived at the large Indian village of Cotapampas in the foothills of the Andes Mountains, where they found gold and jewels in great quantities, but the greedy Pizarro wanted more. Using torture, he learned from the Cotapampas citizens that the principal Inca stronghold of Cajamarca, six hundred miles to the northwest, was a storehouse for gold, silver, and emeralds. Fascinated with the possibility of attaining this great wealth for the Spanish crown, Pizarro forced several of the Cotapampas Indians to guide his force to that city.

On November 15, 1532, Pizarro and his men took up positions around the gates of Cajamarca, an Incan city of some two thousand citizens. Sending his priest and an interpreter to the gate, he demanded an audience with Atahuallpa, the Incan ruler. When Atahuallpa appeared, he was told to immediately accept the Christian teachings of the Spaniards, to acknowledge the King of Spain as the ruler of the world, to lay down his arms, and to turn over his entire fortune to Pizarro. Following the interpretation of these words, the priest proffered the Bible to Atahuallpa. The inference was that, if the Incan leader accepted the book, then he agreed to the demands.

Incensed, Atahuallpa hurled the Bible to the ground and retreated into his city. As the priest retrieved the book, the interpreter returned to Pizarro and described the confrontation and response.

Within minutes, Pizarro sounded the battle cry, and the Spaniards crashed through the gates of Cajamarca, initiating one of the bloodiest slaughters in South American history. In spite of being vastly outnumbered, the far better armed and trained Spaniards completely subdued the city after brisk fighting. Hundreds of Incan warriors were slain and hundreds more imprisoned only to be horribly tortured and killed before the week was over.

Atahuallpa was even taken prisoner and brought before Pizarro. Placing the leader in heavy chains, Pizarro ordered runners sent throughout the countryside informing the natives that if they were to save their ruler's life they were to turn over all of their gold and silver as ransom. Journals kept by Pizarro's secretary claimed that this ransom was to be of sufficient quantity to fill three rooms—each twenty-two feet by seventeen feet, and as tall as a man could reach. The Indians were given two months to comply with the demand.

Because Atahuallpa was a beloved man among the Incas, the citizens lost little time in collecting the gold and silver and giving it to the Spaniards. One of Atahuallpa's soldiers, an Incan named Rumiani, was sent northward to Quito with a small party of warriors and a pack train of llamas to retrieve that city's gold and silver wealth. When Rumiani did not return at the appointed time, Pizarro sent a military detail with a dozen men to that city to ascertain the reason for the delay and hasten the delivery of the wealth. Along with this platoon of soldiers, Pizarro also sent the priest and interpreter to speed up the treasure gathering.

As a result of misunderstandings and misinformation, the citizens of Quito refused to allow Rumiani to take their gold.

Fighting broke out, and warfare in the streets of the city was still raging when the Spanish soldiers arrived several days later.

When the rioting was finally quelled, the llamas were loaded with gold, silver, and precious gems, and arrangements were made to return to Cajamarca. The Spanish captain commanding the expedition, however, began to cast greedy eyes upon the great fortune he watched being loaded onto the pack animals and he made surreptitious arrangements to escape with a portion of it for himself. Taking into his confidence only six of the twelve soldiers who accompanied him to Quito, the captain revealed his plans.

Instead of returning to Cajamarca, the captain intended to travel northward with a portion of the fortune, far from the land of the Incas and into the new and wild country he had heard about from the Indians. He wished to get so far away that pursuit by Pizarro would not be a consideration.

The captain sent six llamas, fully loaded with treasure, on its way to Cajamarca. This pack train was accompanied by the six soldiers who were not a part of the officer's plans. He ordered them to inform Pizarro that the second pack train would follow in just a few days. The captain waited until this caravan was well along the trail toward Cajamarca when he ordered the second one northward. In addition to the six soldiers he enlisted, the captain brought along several Incas to accompany them and tend to the llamas. The priest, an unwilling participant in the theft and desertion, traveled along with this renegade party. The priest walked at the rear of the rich pack train, always clutching his Bible close to his chest.

Meanwhile, in spite of receiving the entire amount of ransom he demanded, Pizarro had Atahuallpa strangled in front of his subjects. The commander then proceeded to travel throughout the Incan kingdom attacking and sacking each and every city he encountered, adding to the tremendous store of wealth he would eventually ship back to Spain. Pizarro was so occupied with his own military activities that he apparently gave little thought to the desertions of several of his soldiers and the priest. In any event, he made no attempt to follow and apprehend them.

No one knows how long the escaping soldiers traveled the prehistoric trade route that wound through the high mountains and deep valleys of the Andes Mountains, along coastlines, across deserts, and up through Central America and Mexico into the unexplored country of Texas. Along the way, the party encountered many villages populated by friendly Indians, who provided food and directions. For many days, they traveled through regions of extreme drought; other times they were subjected to monsoon-like rains. They suffered hardship, disease, starvation, and thirst, but they endured. The continual fear—being pursued by the bloodthirsty Pizarro—hung over them like perpetual storm clouds. This perceived threat kept them on the trail, ever alert, and continually heading northward into some unknown country where, with their great fortune, they intended to establish their own kingdom.

During the entire course of the journey, the Spanish captain compiled a map and journal in order to keep a record of their progress. The map was on a large piece of rawhide, and the inscriptions were burned onto it each evening using coals from the campfire.

One day, untold months following the hurried departure from Quito, the party arrived in what is often referred to as the Double Mountain country of Stonewall County, Texas, a reference to the most prominent landmark in the vicinity. Double Mountain is between the present-day city of Aspermont and the Double Mountain Fork of the Brazos River.

When they first arrived in this area, the travelers discovered they were being watched and followed by Indians. Extremely nervous and uncertain of what to expect, the Spaniards and Incas kept close together and maintained a vigilant eye on the landscape.

Traveling north of Double Mountain, the party stopped to make camp and rest. They camped, it is believed, on the banks of the Salt Fork of the Brazos River.

The captain, fearing an attack by the Indians, decided to unload the treasure from the llamas and bury it nearby. When it was safe to do so, he explained, they would return to this site and retrieve the wealth.

The captain assigned his men to excavate a total of twenty-one deep holes, and into each a portion of the treasure was placed. As the last of the holes was being filled, the priest placed his Bible, carefully wrapped and bound in a piece of soft leather, atop the pile of treasure. Following this, the soldiers led the llamas back and forth across the surface several times, obliterating any indication of the recent excavations. That evening as he sat next to the campfire, the captain recorded the locations of each of the twenty-one caches onto the rawhide map. For several days the party of Spaniards, along with their Inca helpers, remained in the region resting and making plans to travel to a more agreeable climate.

It was never known exactly what became of the group of deserters, for the record of their journey appears to come to an end at the campground on the Salt Fork of the Brazos. It is believed by some researchers that the party fell prey to Indian attack not long after burying the treasure. All were apparently killed, leaving no one who could identify the location of the fabulous cache of gold, silver, jewels, and the precious Bible. Evidence for this conclusion has been provided by the discovery of several skeletons and Spanish artifacts such as armor, weapons, and tools, all found in the late 1800s near Kiowa Peak in the northeastern part of Stonewall County. It is unclear what became of the rawhide map, for it was not found among the remains. It did, however, appear many years later.

Following the Civil War, this part of Texas began to attract settlers who came to ranch. As more and more people moved into the area, the legend of the buried Incan treasure in Stonewall County was told and retold among the residents. A few half-hearted attempts were made to locate the huge cache, but nothing was ever found.

Interest in the Incan treasure was revived in 1876 with the arrival of an elderly Spaniard. Traveling in an elaborate carriage pulled by two stately horses and accompanied by a manservant, the old fellow quietly bought up several parcels of land along the Salt Fork. The few settlers who lived in the area presumed the old man was going to establish a ranch, but after the passage of several weeks it became clear that ranching was not on his mind at all. The Spaniard moved into a tent he had erected on his property, rarely came into a settlement to purchase supplies, and behaved mysteriously. On the few occasions he was observed in town, the Spaniard always possessed what appeared to be a large and rather old rawhide map that he never ceased to study.

After living there for several months, the Spaniard disappeared as suddenly as he had arrived. Following his departure, several neighboring ranchers entered his property to investigate. They found the canvas tent in which the newcomer had lived, now torn to rags by the incessant winds. Here and there they found abandoned tools—shovels, picks, buckets—and not far from the tent site, the men discovered ten freshly dug holes! The ranchers reported the holes were quite deep, and each bore evidence of having contained crates and packs.

No one knows what became of the Spaniard. Did he in fact recover a large portion of the buried Incan treasure? All of the available evidence points toward the possibility that he did. And what about the remaining eleven holes that were described on the rawhide map by the Spanish soldier more than four hundred and fifty years ago?

While a few old-timers in Stonewall County claim to know where the ten excavations were made, decades of sandstorms, flash floods, and other continual and eternal erosion processes, which shape the desert landscape, have long since obliterated any sign of them.

Shortly after the turn of the century, another Spaniard arrived in Stonewall County, this one much younger than the first and also carrying an ancient rawhide map. Though it can probably never be proven, many believed it was the same rawhide map brought into the region a quarter of a century earlier by the previous visitor. Speculation also circulated that the recent newcomer was a relative of the other, perhaps a son.

After spending several days on the property purchased by the first Spaniard, the younger one traveled to the nearest town, purchased a supply of tools and provisions, and hired four men to do some digging for him.

The laborers reported later that they followed the young Spaniard to the area of the Salt Fork where they spent several days observing him studying landmarks and constantlyeferring to the old map that he never let out of his sight. Finally, he provided the workers with instructions on where to excavate.

Within minutes, the workers excavated four skeletons in one of the holes indicated by their employer, but nothing more was found. At other locations, the men dug holes as deep as twelve feet with negative results.

On the day the diggers were to be paid, the young Spaniard told them he had insufficient funds but offered to cut them in on a share of the treasure he believed they would eventually uncover.

After several more days of digging in the hot summer sun and finding nothing, the workers grew hostile and threatened their employer. One evening, the terrified man gathered up his map and few belongings and fled from the area, never to be seen again.

There are many who believe the newcomer had actually found the site of the buried Incan treasure, but the holes he had excavated were probably the same ones dug into by the older Spaniard.

In 1909, an elderly, overweight man with considerable mining experience arrived in the Double Mountain area. Like the two Spaniards who had preceded him, he possessed a map. The one he carried, however, was on parchment, not rawhide. The man's name was David Arnold, and he quietly explored the region looking for certain landmarks noted on his map.

After living in the area for several months, Arnold made an amazing discovery—he found a rock near the confluence of the Double Mountain Fork and the Salt Fork that appeared to have a map inscribed on its surface. The map contained several markings that suggested Spanish origin and coincided with markings on his own map. Some Spanish artifacts were even found nearby.

Because the rock map portrayed a series of lines extending from a central point, it has become known as the "Spider Rock," and is strongly linked to the caching of the Incan treasure. Over the years, other Spider Rocks have been discovered in this region and several researchers continue to try and interpret the markings, but at this writing the mysterious stones have remained undeciphered.

In his late seventies, Arnold's physical infirmities, along with a troublesome divorce he was undergoing, prevented him from continuing his search for the fabulous treasure cache, and he eventually had to abandon his quest.

About three years later, a former wolf hunter named Walter Leach from Rotan came to the region to hunt for the treasure.

Like Arnold, he concentrated his search near the confluence of the Salt and Double Mountain Forks of the Brazos River. Though the multi-million dollar Incan hoard eluded him, Leach did discover a cache of gold that eventually netted around $12,000. Along with the gold, he also found several Spanish artifacts. During the next several months, Leach found other smaller caches of gold and silver, but none as large as the first.

In 1920, Frank D. Olmstead, a wealthy farmer, somehow came into possession of the rawhide map. Olmstead claimed he purchased the item, along with a second map, from a Spanish priest during a vacation in California. Intrigued by the maps, Olmstead began to study everything he could find concerning the lost Incan treasure. Completely captivated by this tale and fascinated by the possibility of recovering the great wealth he believed lay cached underground near the Salt Fork, Olmstead moved to the area, purchased several hundred acres of land, and undertook a prolonged search for the treasure that lasted twenty-eight years.

Olmstead once told a confidant that he would gladly give up the entire Incan treasure if he could only get his hands on the Bible believed to be buried with the hoard. Eventually, he acquired the same plot of land owned by the Spaniard. Thousands of holes were excavated throughout the property, but none yielded anything of value. Olmstead died when he was sixty-three years old and is buried on his property. In death, it is possible he may repose atop one of the rich caches he sought for so long and hard during his lifetime.

The treasure of the Incas, at least a portion of it, is still hidden somewhere in the rough and broken country of Stonewall County near the Salt Fork of the Brazos River, but only the ghosts of the Spaniards know where.

The Rifle Pits

Somewhere in Ochiltree County in the northeastern part of the Texas Panhandle exists a buried treasure of a different type—hundreds of 1860s vintage United States Army rifles, ammunition, sabres, saddles, bottles, cannons, and other military goods. The cache is known to be somewhere near Palo Duro Creek, but in recent times the exact location has become a puzzle for those who continue to search for the valuable hoard.

The Medicine Lodge Treaty of 1867 was like many such agreements between white settlers and Indians in that both sides virtually ignored it. Because of the treaty's failure and the subsequent military responses following a series of Indian attacks, the United States Army assigned hundreds of soldiers and cavalrymen into the field to round up the insurgents who fled from the reservations and spread out across the plains.

On December 1, 1868, General Eugene A. Carr took command of the Fifth Cavalry Regiment at Fort Lyon, Colorado. This group was soon joined by the Tenth Cavalry, eventually totaling seven hundred soldiers along with service and supply personnel.

Under Carr's direction, the Fifth Regiment received orders to march southward in search of renegade Indians. The soldiers had not been on the trail long when a severe blizzard struck. Blizzards are not uncommon in this part of the country, but this one descended on the area earlier in the season than usual, and, according to the old-timers in this area, was the worst storm in at least fifty years. Between the blinding snow and temperatures that often plummeted below zero, Carr's command was often forced to seek shelter. Sometimes they were able to pitch camp in the protective cover of a dense grove of trees, but more often than not they were caught out on the open prairie. When this occurred, the troopers had difficulty erecting tents because the strong winds blew them down. Once, Carr ordered the soldiers to construct dugouts, but the ground was frozen solid and could not be penetrated by their shovels.

The severe storm had extremely slowed the movement of the command, and by the time they reached a specified rendezvous point they had nearly run out of provisions. Carr had counted on wild game and buffalo to provide some meat for the troop, but the blinding storm made hunting very difficult.

One of Carr's scouts was William F. Cody, who later gained fame as "Buffalo Bill." Realizing the gravity of his predicament, Carr dispatched Cody to forage ahead and select a suitable location for camp, one that could serve for several weeks. After a full day of scouting, Cody returned and led the large force of cavalrymen to a location next to Palo Duro Creek, a small stream of clear water that bisected the county in a southwest to northeast direction. Here fresh water ran and a grove of hardwoods could provide wood for fuel and some simple fortifications. As the soldiers bent to the task of setting up camp, Cody, gathering several other hunters and scouts about him, departed to search for buffalo.

Because Carr believed they would likely remain at this site for several weeks, he supervised the excavation of several deep dugouts in the prairie soil to be used to store the arms and other supplies and protect them from the elements. He placed hundreds of rifles, sabres, saddles, bridles, several cannons, numerous boxes of ammunition, full bottles of whiskey, and two wagons into these dugouts .

From this crude camp on the wind- and snow-swept Texas plains, Carr, as dictated by his orders, sent out platoons of soldiers in search of Indians. Originally, Carr's troopers were to be continually resupplied by other regiments moving through the area, but the terrible storm created difficulties with the timing. Patrols came and went, no Indians were ever sighted, and provisions continued to run dangerously low.

After several days of hunting, Cody finally succeeded in providing the soldiers with fresh antelope and buffalo meat. While he and his hunters butchered meat from several carcasses, Cody spotted an eastbound Mexican pack train carrying a load of trade goods to St. Louis. Among the cargo was a large quantity of food and beer, so the scout diverted the caravan from its course and led it to the campsite.

Every few days, Carr received messages from other commands in the region. Like Carr's force, all of them battled the storm but were ordered to remain where they were encamped until receiving further instructions.

Carr and his men were eager to encounter Indians and the idle waiting, along with the extremely cold weather, began to make them edgy and irritable. Days turned into weeks, and instead of letting up, the storm grew progressively worse. There was seldom a time when the ground was not covered with six to eight inches of snow. Game was growing scarce and Cody and the other scouts were finding it more and more difficult to provide the seven hundred men with fresh meat. The supply of firewood began to thin.

As the food supplies gradually ran low and the weather failed to improve, most of the civilian service and supply personnel abandoned the encampment and returned to Colorado. In addition, the horses and mules had eaten all of the available forage and were now dying of starvation and cold. Scurvy also broke out among the soldiers, and the regiment physician told Carr something must be done soon or it would be necessary to abandon the camp.

The situation grew bleaker by the day, then Cody finally located a large herd of buffalo. In a short time, he and his hunters killed more than a hundred of the shaggy creatures, returned to the camp with plenty of fresh meat, and saved Carr's command from starvation. Cody was regarded by all of the soldiers as a hero, and it was at this time that his fame and reputation as a hunter and scout began to escalate.

The worst of the hardship was over. Carr eventually received orders to abandon the encampment immediately and return to Fort Lyon. Because he had lost so many horses and mules to the blizzard, he did not have enough stock to pull the wagons, which would have transported the war material stored in the earthen dugouts.

Frustrated, Carr decided to cave in the dugouts, effectively burying the material, and planned to return for it with another expedition when the weather grew warmer. As the cavalry force rode northward, abandoning the area, hundreds of rifles, ammunition, other military hardware, along with bottled and canned drink and remaining foodstuffs lay buried under several inches of prairie earth.

Following his return to Fort Lyon, Carr received orders to lead another expedition to the west and was never able to return to Texas to retrieve the material buried near Palo Duro Creek. Eventually, the army decided it was too much trouble and promptly forgot about it.

Buffalo hunters who frequented this region throughout much of the 1870s often established camps near the old military dugouts on Palo Duro Creek. The buffalo hunters knew of the caches and referred to them as the "rifle pits." Because the cavalry armament and other equipment was useless for hunting buffalo, the caches were ignored. The term "rifle pits," however, entered the language and to this day is used to identify the old caved-in dugouts.

Early settlers were also aware of the rifle pits but were too busy trying to maintain their herds of cattle and coaxing crops out of the semi-arid ground to worry about what was in the abandoned holes.

As time passed, the prairie changed. Natural processes altered the landscape as did new settlements across the region. During the 1970s, a treasure hunter came to Palo Duro Creek in Ochiltree County searching for the rifle pits. While exploring the area, he found a rock inscribed with the name "W. F. Cody." The treasure hunter determined that somewhere nearby must lie the buried fortune in historical military armament and equipment, but several days of searching and digging yielded nothing.

The ranchers and farmers who live in this region today maintain that no one has ever found the rifle pits. Some say the region has grassed over and the land eroded and changed to the degree that the actual site of the rifle pits cannot be identified. Others claim that Palo Duro Creek shifted its course and the cache is no longer near the bank but perhaps several dozen yards away.

Regardless of the changes, the fact remains that an 1870s military cache containing what may amount to more than a million dollars' worth of antique guns, sabres, bottles, and other material remains hidden beneath just a few inches of Panhandle prairie soil in Ochiltree County.

Lost Texas Ranger Treasure

During the embryonic days of the famed Texas Rangers, new recruits were desperately needed and most were little more than seventeen- and eighteen-year-old farmer boys. Scattered among this youth and raw inexperienced were occasionally found some older men of dubious reputation—former outlaws.

Fergus Dooley was one such man. Dooley had migrated to Texas from Indiana as a young man and immediately discovered the easy profits from stolen cattle and horses. Assembling a small but aggressive gang of rustlers, Dooley preyed upon the many small and large ranches throughout central and south Texas. Though it was never proven, many believed that Dooley had killed several men.

Vigilante patrols eventually put Dooley out of the rustling business forcing him to find another way to earn a living. While riding through the bustling town of Austin one day, he spotted a notice tacked to the door of a mercantile that called for men to join the newly formed Texas Rangers. With nothing better to do and almost broke, Dooley decided to sign up. Within the week, Dooley was commanding a Ranger company, an ill-disciplined group of young boys whose previous captain had been shot through the head by an Indian.

One morning, Dooley was handed orders to lead his youthful troop of twelve recruits, who had been Rangers for no longer than two months, about sixty miles west to the town of Fredericksburg.

Ironically, Dooley's Ranger detachment would provide protection to the settlers from cattle rustlers.

Leaving Austin at dawn, the Rangers spent an entire day in the saddle and covered nearly thirty miles. By sunset, Dooley and his young Rangers were tired and hungry and sought a suitable campsite with water and graze for the horses. Just as he was about to give up finding a decent campsite, Dooley spotted a campfire up ahead near the trail and decided to approach it.

Riding into a grove of trees near a small creek, Dooley's Rangers encountered a party of eight Mexicans sitting around the fire playing cards. A stack of gold coins was next to each man. At the noisy arrival of the Rangers, the Mexicans leaped to their feet, grabbed their rifles, and held them at the ready, pointing straight toward the newcomers.

As Dooley rode up to the group, he spotted two freight wagons parked back in the trees and several fine horses hobbled and grazing on the grass near the creek.

Dooley waved, smiled a greeting to the Mexicans, dismounted, and approached the leader. He explained he and his men had been riding all day and were tired and, if it were not considered an intrusion, would like to camp nearby. Perceiving the newcomers to be friendly, the Mexicans lowered their guns and the leader welcomed them into the camp, even inviting them to share some dinner.

After a meal of venison and wild onions, the Mexicans invited Dooley to play cards with them. While the recruits busied them-selves with setting up camp about fifty yards away, Dooley sat down to several rounds of monte. During the card games, Dooley learned that the Mexicans had departed Austin just ahead of the Rangers and were returning to their homes in west Texas. In Austin, they had sold a large herd of horses and mules along with two wagonloads of goods. They were returning, said the leader, with more than $40,000 in gold coins, profit from the sales and collections earned from previous business transactions. As he spoke, the leader held a handful of the coins above the ground, letting them slide slowly through his fingers to clink noisily against each other on the saddle blanket upon which he sat.

After playing cards for about two hours, Dooley lost what little money he carried. As he was returning to his camp, he was struck with an idea. He decided to kill the Mexicans and take their gold.

Entering the Ranger camp, he told his charges that the band of Mexicans playing cards by the fire were notorious horse thieves wanted in Texas. Later, when the Mexicans fell asleep, he told the Rangers, they would enter the camp and kill them all.

About two hours before sunrise, the Rangers, led by Dooley, crept toward the Mexican camp. On a signal from the leader, the young Rangers fired into the bedrolls of the sleepers, killing them all.

When the smoke cleared and Dooley was certain the Mexicans were dead, he instructed his Rangers to return to the camp and get some sleep before riding out later. When the last of them departed, Dooley began searching the wagons for gold. After several minutes, he discovered a dozen canvas sacks filled with coins. Placing the sacks into stout leather saddlebags, he tied them securely onto two of the Mexicans' horses and selected a fine mount for himself. While the Rangers were preparing to bed down for a few hours, Dooley quietly mounted and led the pack horses, loaded with gold, out of the camp and northwest along a dim trail toward Abilene.

After passing through Abilene, Dooley continued on in the hope of reaching Colorado before the start of winter. During the entire journey from the campground to Abilene, he did not see a single traveler, but after leaving the rough and rowdy west Texas town, Dooley became aware of Indians constantly watching him from afar.

Each day the number of Comanches who trailed Dooley increased, and by the time he reached the Double Mountain Fork of the Brazos River there were twelve mounted warriors who rode parallel to his route, always remaining about two hundred yards away. At night, Dooley was too frightened to sleep and would remain close to his campfire, the saddlebags filled with gold coins stacked nearby.

After several more days of riding, Dooley arrived at the huge canyon cut into the soft High Plains limestone by the Prairie Dog Town Fork of the Red River, the canyon that came to be known as Palo Duro. He and his horses were weary from the long journey, but the outlaw was anxious to cross the huge gorge and reach the other side. After riding hundreds of yards in either direction along the canyon's rim, Dooley failed to locate a suitable descent down the steep slope. Frustrated, he decided to follow the canyon rim in the upstream direction, believing he would eventually encounter a crossing.

The next morning after breaking camp and loading the sacks of gold onto the spare horses, Dooley spotted the Comanches, closer now than before. Their number had grown to fifteen, all of them painted and seated upon their ponies aligned in a row facing the Ranger. Fearing an attack but realizing he was virtually defenseless against this many armed warriors, Dooley slowly mounted and, taking the lead ropes of the pack animals, continued riding along the rim. The Indians followed, matching his pace.

Around noon, Dooley decided to stop and prepare lunch. As he built a small fire, he considered that the Comanches might only want to trade horses. He decided to make some coffee and invite the leader of the Indians to join him for a parley. As he built up the fire and added some coffee to the metal pot, the line of warriors spread out into a wide semicircle about fifty yards away. With the deep canyon at his back and the Indians to his front, Dooley realized he was trapped.

Suddenly, and without warning, the Indians charged. While three of the Comanches grabbed Dooley's startled horses, the remainder swooped down on the surprised Ranger, impaling him with a dozen arrows and several lances. As he fell on the coals of the fire, Dooley screamed for mercy and thrashed about in painful agony. While he was still alive, an Indian cut the scalp from his head. When death finally ended his screams, Dooley was dragged to the edge of the canyon wall and thrown into the gorge below.

The warriors who captured Dooley's horses cut the saddlebags from their backs, letting them fall to the ground. One of the Comanches tore open the bags and cut into one of the canvas sacks. Having no use at all for the white man's money, the Indian threw the gold coins to the ground and abandoned the saddlebags where they lay.

Moments later as the Comanches rode away from the bloody scene, the Panhandle winds blew tiny grains of sand up against the bulk of the gold-filled saddlebags. Days later, Dooley's skeleton, picked clean by buzzards, ravens, coyotes, and insects, gleamed white in the sun at the bottom of the canyon. On the rim above the remains of Fergus Dooley's final campfire, small portions of the exposed leather saddlebags could still be seen, not yet covered by the constantly shifting sand. The coins lay in the canvas sacks, a few on the ground, and all gradually disappearing under the wind-blown sands.

Fergus Dooley's treasure in gold coins still lies somewhere today close to the edge of the south rim of Palo Duro Canyon.

Shafter Lake's Wagonloads of Gold

One of the most curious cases of lost treasure on the Great Plains is that associated with Shafter Lake, a sometimes dry depression in the arid Texas landscape just a few miles northwest of Andrews. The origin and destination of the tremendous amount of gold reputedly lost in this lake remains unknown to this day, and although great mystery surrounds this huge treasure, it may actually be one of the most attainable lost fortunes on the Great Plains.

William Rufus Shafter was born on October 16, 1835, the first white baby to be born in Michigan, according to historians. At the onset of the Civil War, Shafter enlisted with the Seventh Michigan Infantry and saw action at Ball's Bluff, Yorktown, West Point, Fair Oaks, and Nashville, where he was wounded. Following the war, General George Henry Thomas, the "Rock of Chickamauga," praised Shafter, who was given the assignment of commanding black troops on the Texas frontier. During this time, Shafter picked up the nickname "Pecos Bill," and quickly earned a reputation as a tough commander and fierce fighter.

As a result of obscure references and some undocumented military reports discovered in 1957, many believe that Pecos Bill Shafter and a contingent of soldiers were involved in escorting two wagonloads of gold from Mexico to some unknown destination in the United States. The gold's origins, value, and destination have remained a mystery to this day. Ongoing research into military files has yielded no pertinent information whatsoever.

As the story goes, Shafter and his party, along with the two wagonloads of gold, had just skirted the treacherous sand dunes located near the present-day town of Monahans and were traveling in a northeasterly direction when one of the scouts spotted a band of approximately forty Comanches following one mile behind the group. During this time, the Comanches were active in raiding settlements and ranches and were known to attack and kill travelers in the region. To guard against attack, Shafter placed several well-armed riders at the rear of the caravan and pushed on until evening when he ordered camp near what is now Notrees, Texas. It was a nervous encampment that night as most of the soldiers kept a wary eye out for hostile Indians.

After a quick breakfast, the caravan set forth once again across the arid Texas plains, the Indians trailing behind. All day long the two wagons and the armed escort continued on a direct northeasterly course. Their progress was occasionally slowed by deep arroyos and washed-out trails. As evening approached, Shafter once again ordered camp, this time near the southwestern shore of a large playa in present-day Andrews County.

Playas are naturally occurring lake beds usually found in arid and semi-arid environments. They are normally dry and exhibit a crusty soil—the residue of salt deposition resulting from intense evaporation of saline-laden runoff. During the time of year that Shafter and his troops were escorting the gold across the plains, rainfall was unseasonably high, making travel difficult at times, and occasionally filling up many of the playas.

As the troops dined on cold provisions that evening, Shafter and a sergeant examined the lake and estimated it to be no deeper than three or four feet. Rather than use up valuable time riding around the large playa, Shafter decided to cut through it on the morrow.

The next morning, after the teams were hitched to the wagons and the soldiers mounted, Shafter waved the party forward into the playa. Entering the quiet, saline waters of the shallow lake, the horses and wagons generated ripples that lapped just above the axles.

Near the center of the playa, trouble developed. The lead wagon became mired in the soft bottom and came to a complete halt. As the second wagon stopped behind the first, it too began to sink into the saturated sands and silts of the lake bed. Extra horses were added to the teams, but to no avail. Both wagons were hopelessly stuck.

As Shafter pondered his predicament, the troops saw the Comanches on the southwestern shore. After regarding the milling soldiers for several minutes, the leader of the Indians yelled a great whoop, and the painted attackers swarmed into the playa after the soldiers. Abandoning the wagons, Shafter and his troopers fled to the far shore and escaped across the dry plains.

The Comanches pursued the soldiers for four miles before abandoning the chase. Returning to the wagons in the lake, the Indians searched for anything useful, taking only the tarpaulins and rope and setting fire to the vehicles. As the wagon beds' wooden planks burned away, the heavy loads of gold broke through and dropped into the water and onto the saturated floor of the soft lake bed.

Because white men rarely traveled this part of Texas, the two wagons gradually rotted away unnoticed during successive years, their parts falling to the playa's floor and becoming part of the debris already settled there.

According to available military records, Shafter and his command never retrieved the gold, which, after the passage of time, no doubt settled at some depth below the floor of the soft lake bed. Pecos Bill Shafter went on to other glories in the army, eventually leading a contingent of troops at the 1898 Santiago Campaign in Cuba. He died in 1906.

Many researchers claim that Shafter was involved with illegally transporting a fortune in gold that he intended to make his own out of Mexico. A few Shafter scholars dispute this contention and suggest that he was on a clandestine mission for the army that possibly involved delivering the gold to a secret military treasury. Whatever the reason, legend claims the treasure was lost in what eventually became known as Shafter Lake.

In 1901, William Russell, his wife, and three sons were traveling from Denton, Texas, to the Pecos River Valley where they hoped to establish a farm and orchard. Near Andrews, the Russell wagon broke down, and several days passed while repairs were made. While Russell worked on the disabled wagon, his boys played nearby in the dry lake bed. During dinner one evening, Russell observed his boys involved in a game with some items he had never seen. On examining the items, he found them to be wagon parts. After asking the boys where they found the items, the youngsters pointed out toward the middle of the playa. The next morning Russell, curious, walked out into the dry lake bed and found several more rotted pieces of at least two wagons. He was completely unaware that mere inches beneath his feet reposed an incredible treasure of gold.

Almost ten years later, Russell told a friend about finding the wagon parts in the dry lake bed. The friend immediately related the story of Shafter's lost treasure and Russell realized at that point a fortune was hidden in the playa. Taking time off from his farming, Russell, two of his sons, and a neighbor returned to

Shafter Lake to try to relocate the rotted wagon debris. By this time, however, the remainder of the wagon parts had either rotted completely away or were buried by the blowing, shifting sands and salts of the lake bed. Though the four men spent several days searching the playa, they were unsuccessful in finding the site. Russell returned to his farm and never attempted to locate the Shafter Lake treasure again.

In 1931, an Andrews rancher reported finding several pieces of an old wagon "out in the middle of Lake Shafter." When he related his discovery in town, several who were familiar with the legend went out to the lake but found nothing.

In normal years, occasional west Texas rainfall and associated runoff leave water standing for a time in Shafter Lake. The water eventually evaporates and infiltrates into the porous soil quickly. Each time the lake bed becomes saturated, the soil expands, allowing any heavy particles or objects that might be lying upon it to gradually sink into the wet muck. It was thus that the gold transported by Pecos Bill Shafter disappeared into the playa and from all accounts and evidence, it is still there.

How deep into the lake bed the gold has sunk is open to conjecture. Most researchers say it is likely not more than two to three feet. A few estimate it could be as much as four feet deep. Because of the relatively remote location of Shafter Lake, few have attempted any kind of sophisticated recovery attempt. An enterprising individual or group possessing patience, time, energy, and a good metal detector, however, might possibly recover this long-lost and legendary golden treasure.

Glossary

- **Arable:** Fit for cultivation by plowing or tillage.
- **Auger:** A tool used for boring a hole in soil or wood.
- **Blunderbuss:** An obsolete short firearm having a large bore and usually a flaring muzzle.
- **Breechclout:** Also breechcloth. A cloth or leather worn in warm weather to cover the loins.
- **Buckboard:** A four-wheeled vehicle with a spring-supported platform.
- **Bullion:** Uncoined gold or silver in bars or ingots.
- **Cache:** A hiding place for concealing implements, provisions, or money.
- **Chock:** A wedge or block used for inhibiting the movement of a wheel.
- **Colony:** A body of people living in a new territory but with retaining ties to the parent state; the actual territory inhabited by such a body.
- **Confiscate:** To appropriate; to take from someone.
- **Corral:** A pen or enclosure for confining livestock.
- **Dugout:** A shelter dug into a hillside or the ground and roofed with sod; used for quarters, storage, or protection.
- **Escarpment:** A log cliff or steep slope separating two comparatively level or more gently sloping surfaces; generally resulting from erosion or faulting.
- **Excavation:** A cavity or hole formed from digging or scooping.
- **Fascism:** A political philosophy or movement that exalts nation and race above the individual and that stands for a central autocratic government headed by a dictatorial leader. Generally accompanied by severe social and economic regimentation.

- **Fault:** A fracture in the earth's crust accompanied by displacement on one side with respect to the other.

- **Feedlot:** A plot of land on which livestock are fattened for market.

- **Flintlock:** A type of gun; specifically, a lock for a rifle or pistol having a flint in the hammer for striking a spark to ignite the charge.

- **Gunwales:** The upper edge of the side of a boat or ship; formerly used as a support for guns.

- **Hasp:** A device for fastening a door or lid consisting of a hinged metal strap that fits over a staple and is secured by pin or padlock.

- **Highwayman:** A person who robs travelers on a road.

- **Ingot:** A mass of metal cast into a convenient shape for storage or transportation.

- **Inter:** To deposit a body in the earth or a tomb.

- **Lance:** A steel- or stone-tipped spear normally carried by a mounted warrior or knight.

- **Livery:** Also livery stable. A business establishment devoted to the feeding, caring, and stabling of horses for pay; a concern offering vehicles for rent.

- **Magnate:** A person of rank, power, influence, or distinction, often in a specified area.

- **Mercantile:** Relating to merchants or trading. A term often used for a place of business that sells hardware and other supplies.

- **Mint:** A place where coins, metals, or tokens are made.

- **Monte:** A card game in which players select any two of four cards turned face up in a layout and bet that one of them will be matched before the other as cards are dealt one at a time from the deck.

- **Mule skinner:** Also muleteer. One who drives mules.

- **Ore:** A mineral containing a valuable constituent for which it is mined and worked.

- **Pack train:** A line of horses, mules, or burros which are packed with goods for transportation.

- **Parabola:** A plane curve generated by a point moving so that its distance from a fixed point is equal to its distance from a fixed line.

- **Pediment:** A broad, gently sloping bedrock surface with low relief and situated at the base of a steeper slope. The foothills.

- **Platoon:** A subdivision of a company-size military unit normally consisting of two or more squads or sections.

- **Playa:** A shallow, undrained basin occasionally holding water. Often found in arid lands.

- **Pleistocene:** A geologic epoch, normally associated with the Ice Age.

- **Posse:** A body of persons summoned by a sheriff to assist in preserving the public peace, usually in an emergency.

- **Post:** Military; a place where soldiers are stationed.

- **Prow:** The pointed, projected front part of a ship.

- **Ravine:** A narrow, steep-sided valley, larger than a gully and smaller than a canyon. Formed as a result of erosion by running water.

- **Recluse:** A person who leads a secluded or solitary life.

- **Reverie:** To daydream; to be lost in thought.

- **Runoff:** That portion of rain water or melted snow on the land that flows over the surface and normally reaches a stream at a lower level.

- **Saddlebags:** A pair of covered pouches laid across the back of a horse behind the saddle.

- **Sediment:** Fine-grained sands, silts, and clays carried and deposited by winds, flowing water, or glaciers.

- **Sedimentary:** Of, relating to, or containing sediment. Layered rock formed from deposition.

- **Sod:** Grass-covered surface of the ground; to cover with sod or turf.

- **Specie:** Money in the form of coin.

- **Stage:** Also stagecoach. a horse-drawn passenger and mail coach running on a regular schedule between established stops.

- **Stockyard:** A place where cattle, sheep, swine, or horses are kept temporarily for slaughter, market, or shipping.

- **Tack shed:** Small building, generally adjacent to a barn, in which saddles, bridles and other stable gear are stored.

- **Tarp:** Short for tarpaulin, a piece of material—usually waterproofed canvas —used for protecting exposed objects.

- **Topography:** The configuration of the surface of the land including relief and position of natural and man-made features.

- **Trace chains:** Parts of a harness used for attaching horse or oxen to a vehicle to be drawn.

- **Utopia:** An imaginery and ideal country.

- **Wallow:** A depression formed as a result of wallowing animals such as buffalo.

- **War club:** A club-shaped implement used as a weapon, especially by American Indians.

Selected References

Carson, Xanthus. "The $63 Million Inca Loot That Landed in West Texas, Part I," *Lost Treasure*. December 1976.

_____. "The $63 Million Inca Loot That Landed in West Texas, Part II," *Lost Treasure*. January 1977.

_____. *Treasure! Bonanzas Worth a Billion Bucks*. San Antonio: The Naylor Company, 1974.

_____. "The Mystery of Choteau's Island," *Treasure*. March 1973.

_____. "The Lost $3,000,000 Wagon Train," *Treasure*. October 1972.

Casey, Tim. "The Black Hills' Lost Stage Loot," *Lost Treasure*. December 1991.

Chrisman, Harry E. *Tales of the Western Heartland*. Athens, Ohio: Ohio University Press, 1984.

Dearen, Patrick. *Portraits of the Pecos Frontier*. Lubbock, Texas: Texas Tech University Press, 1993.

Ferguson, Jeff. "Hijacked Bullion of Central City," *Lost Treasure*. June-July 1975.

Henson, Michael Paul. "North Dakota Treasure," *Lost Treasure*. December 1991.

Holt, Benjamin. "Trader's Lost Mexican Silver," *True Treasure*. March-April 1975.

Hunt, Burl. "The Ice House Treasure," *True Treasure*. November-December 1972.

Jameson, W. C. *Buried Treasures of Texas*. Little Rock: August House Publishers, Inc., 1991.

_____. *Buried Treasures of the American Southwest*. Little Rock: August House Publishers, Inc., 1989.

Larned Collection, North Dakota State Historical Society.

LeGaye, E.S. *Treasure Anthology, Volume I*. Houston: Western Heritage Press, 1973.

Lovelace, Leland. *Lost Mines and Hidden Treasure*. San Antonio: The Naylor Company, 1956.

Steele, Phillip W. *Outlaws and Gunfighter of the Old West*. Springdale, Ark.: Heritage Publishers, 1991.

Townsend, Ben. "Rich Trove Near Lyons, Kansas," *Lost Treasure*. June 1976.

_____. "Missing Loot of the Dalton Gang," *Lost Treasure*. January 1976.

_____. "Outlaw Gold In Kansas," *True Treasure*. March-April 1975.

_____. "Gold Caches at Plattsmouth," *Treasure World*. October-November 1974.

Walker, Dale. *Mavericks: Ten Uncorralled Westerners*. Phoenix: Golden West Publishers, 1989.

Weinmann, Ken. "Doctor Talbott's Lost Keg of Gold Coins," *Lost Treasure*. January 1991.

Wilson, Steve. *Oklahoma Treasure and Treasure Tales*. Norman, Oklahoma: University of Oklahoma Press, 1976.